THE VAMPIRE'S LOVE

OTHER WORLD SERIES BOOK TWO

RAMONA GRAY

EK PUBLISHING INC.

THE VAMPIRE'S LOVE

OTHER WORLD SERIES BOOK TWO

It's been over a year since Val has last seen Abigail. Driven nearly mad by her loss, he finally accepts that she is gone to him forever. Until the night he discovers her about to be sold at a human auction.

After rescuing her from her new captor he is stunned to realize that his little dove is no longer the shy, frightened human she once was. When he learns of her plan to rescue her new human friends from the deadly games they are being forced to participate in, he reluctantly agrees to help her.

Abby is determined to save her friends. Even if it means trusting Val - the vampire she swore she'd never allow to control her again.

Author's Note
This is Book Two in the 'Other World' series and The Vampire's Kiss (Book One) MUST be read first.

Although Book Two tells a complete story, be warned that there is a bit of a cliff-hanger at the end because who doesn't love a good cliff-hanger?

CHAPTER 1

"Care for a drink, Sir? Only a gold coin."

Val looked up at the vampire standing before him. A woman wearing only a skirt and a thin collar around her neck with a chain attached to it, swayed next to him. The vampire tilted her chin up and showed him her throat.

Val wrinkled his nose in disgust. The woman was thin and pale with missing front teeth and stringy black hair. She had multiple bite marks on her neck and upper chest and she was barely conscious.

"No," he grunted and flapped his hand irritably at the vampire. "Leave me."

"Christ, Val. Why do you come to these places if you're not going to drink?" Faren grumbled.

"I wouldn't drink from any of the women in this place. God knows what they carry in their blood," Val snapped.

Faren shrugged. "It's not my fault we can't afford a better dining experience. You're the one who refused to rob the humans we stumbled upon last night."

Val rolled his eyes. "You drank your fill of their blood. Was that not enough for you?"

"If you had let me take those heavy coin purses around their waists, we wouldn't be sitting in a dump like this," Faren remarked.

"Have we not done enough to the humans already? Is it not bad enough that many of our kind kill them for no reason? That we keep them as pets to drink from when we feel like it?"

"I know we've only known each for a few months but your love for the humans is really starting to get on my nerves," Faren said.

"I have no love for them," he snarled. "I just believe we are better off staying away from them."

"Stay away from them?" Faren shook his head. "Have you gone mad? They're our food source remember?"

"There are other ways to live."

Faren snorted. "You mean wildlife? No thanks. Deer are fine when there is nothing else but why bother when there are so many humans available? Hell, half of them want us to bite them."

Faren drummed his fingers on the table. "I still believe the Great War between the vampires and the humans could have been avoided if we had just practiced a little moderation. If we had only drunk from the willing, they may not be so anxious to kill us now."

Val rolled his eyes. "It would have happened regardless. Our kind and their kind were never meant to live in harmony."

Faren stared at him shrewdly. "Tell me, Val, how long has it been since you drank the blood of a human?"

"Thirteen months," he grunted.

Faren whistled under his breath. "Christ, it's a wonder you're still standing."

"Fuck you, Faren."

2

Faren held up his hands. "You know as well as I do that we cannot exist on animal blood forever. We need human blood to be at our full capacity. Can you even lift that sword you carry around your waist?"

"Would you care to find out?" Val asked silkily.

"I do not," Faren said cheerfully. He looked around the crowded room as the auctioneer leaped on to the stage set up against the far wall.

"Ladies and gentlemen! Thank you for your patience! I'm bringing out our next human for auction and I think you'll agree this one has been worth the wait. She is young and strong, and I have a feeling her blood tastes as sweet as honey."

The curtains behind the stage opened and Faren watched with bright interest as a woman was led out. She was naked from the waist up and he whistled appreciatively at the sight of her full breasts. Her bottom half was covered by a short piece of brown fabric and her feet were bare. A leather collar circled her neck and the auctioneer yanked on the thick chain that was attached to it. She stumbled forward and stared at the floor of the stage, her face hidden by her long dark hair.

"Ooh, that's a good one." Faren nudged Val and he gave a brief, disinterested glance at the woman on the stage before looking away.

"She's nice and curvy. So many of them are skinny and fragile now. They last maybe a couple of months before they're too weak for you to feed from. You have to feed them loads of food just to keep them going. Not worth it in my opinion – they're hardly worth the gold you pay for them," Faren said. He licked his lips. "This one though, I'd pay a good amount for her."

"Forget it, Faren. We barely have enough money to find lodging for the day. I'm not sleeping in some dirty cellar just because you want to spend the last of our money on a pet," Val said warningly.

"I suppose you're right," Faren sighed. He took one last look at the woman before glancing at Val. "Ahh, the bug appears."

Violet, her small face peering out from the strands of Val's hair, glared at him and made a rude gesture with her tiny hand.

Faren laughed. "I will never understand why on earth you allow that pest to live in your hair. Why not squash her and be done with it?"

Violet sat down on Val's shoulder. She kept his hair wrapped around her to hide her small body and stared around idly.

"It's none of your business, Faren. I've told you that before," Val growled.

"You are as soft-hearted towards the bug as you are to the humans. I could get rid of her for you if you'd like," Faren offered. "I can make it quick and painless."

"Go anywhere near the little bug and you'll feel the tip of my sword pierce your heart. Do I make myself clear?" Val warned, his hand resting lightly on the handle of his sword.

"Yes, yes. God, Val, I was only joking."

Val relaxed against his chair and ignored the soft kiss that Violet placed on his neck. In the thirteen months since the vampire had taken Abigail, he'd had plenty of opportunity to lose the bug. In the first few weeks, as he searched desperately for Abby, he had barely even noticed the tiny pixie clinging to him. When his head cleared, and the horrible truth set in - Abigail was lost to him forever – he thought about driving the pixie away like he had driven Eone and Neil and Maria away. In the end he couldn't do it. Abigail had loved

Violet dearly and the little pixie was the last part of her that he had to remember her by.

Besides, he had believed the bug would eventually wander away on her own. As the months passed and Violet stuck around, he realized that for her, he was the last part of Abigail that she had left. They had forged an unlikely friendship.

Now, he reached into his pocket and pulled out a small piece of dried meat. He handed it to her without speaking and she took it and chewed on it as she peered around the room.

"Who will start the bidding?" The auctioneer cried merrily from the stage. His fangs flashed in the dim light and he raised his hand. "We will start at twenty-five gold pieces."

Grumbling erupted across the room and the auctioneer bellowed laughter. "Come, come gentlemen. You can see for yourself how delectable she is!" He reached out and cupped one full breast before sliding his hand down her flat stomach. "She alone could feed a family of four for months! Who will give me twenty-five?"

"Over here!" A tall, thin vampire raised his hand and the auctioneer nodded.

"Fifty!"

"Sixty!"

As the bidding increased steadily, Val felt Violet stiffen against his neck. She leaned forward and stared intently at the woman on the stage. He could feel her wings vibrating softly against his neck and he frowned.

"What is it, bug?"

Her eyes wide and her mouth trembling, she stared at him and then pointed to the woman standing with her head bowed.

"What?"

She pointed frantically, and he nodded without really

looking at the woman on the stage. "Yes, I see her. What? You suddenly want a human pet like Faren?"

He snorted soft laughter and turned back to Faren. "We need to find lodging for tomorrow. I do not want it to be like last week where we were forced to dig holes in the ground before the sun burned us to a crisp."

Faren shrugged. "The old ones used to sleep in the ground all the time, Val. We have become soft."

"That may be true but – OW!" He clapped his hand to his neck and stared at the blood on his fingers in disbelief. Violet had bit him hard with her tiny needle-like teeth and he turned his head and glared at the pixie.

"What the hell, bug?"

She yanked on his hair and pointed to the stage again.

He glanced up to see the auctioneer holding his hands up. "Now, gents, before we go any further, I feel I should be truthful. Although the front of her is pleasing to the eye, she does have a bit of scarring on her back. It was probably put there from her last master. Although I dare say she did one of the markings herself. The foolish human tried to protect herself from us with this!"

He swung the woman around and all of the air was sucked from Val's lungs. The woman's back was marred with scars and there was no mistaking the scar of the cross on her lower back.

The woman about to be sold was Abigail.

CHAPTER 2

Violet, her wings fluttering violently, flew off of Val's shoulder toward the stage. Quickly, Val reached out and snagged her tiny leg. She turned and glared at him, struggling to free herself as he pulled her back towards him.

"Not yet, bug," he whispered.

She ignored him and continued to struggle as Faren watched with interest.

"Bug!" Val glared at her. "You cannot help her! Be still for a moment and let me think!"

She stared at his face for a moment and then relaxed. He dropped her back onto his shoulder as he stared at Abigail.

The auctioneer had turned her forward again and Val watched as he grabbed her hair and yanked her head up. She stared vacantly into the crowd as Val's pulse thudded in his veins. Her hair was longer, it trailed nearly to her waist and she had lost weight. Her formerly round belly was now flat and her breasts, while still full, were smaller. Her face had lost its fullness and her arms and legs were thick with muscle.

She continued to stare vacantly into the crowd as the auctioneer called for more bids.

"Faren, how much money do you have?"

Faren shrugged. "About sixty in gold. Why?"

Val cursed softly. The price for Abigail had already gone over a hundred pieces of gold and he didn't have a hope of winning the bidding war for her.

Faren stared at Abigail for a moment and then back at Val. "What? Now you want to buy a human pet?"

Val didn't reply and Faren shook his head. "What has gotten into you, Val?"

"Shut up goddammit!" Val snarled.

He watched as a tall and powerful looking vampire stood up from the back of the room. "Three hundred!"

The auctioneer blinked in surprise and waited a few moments. When no other offered a higher bid, he grinned and shouted, "Sold for three hundred."

The vampire sat down, grinning widely, as Abigail was led off the stage. She disappeared behind the curtain and Val stood up, pulling the hood of his cloak over his head. "We're leaving. Let's go, Faren."

He weaved his way through the crowd towards the door and Faren, shaking his head in confusion, followed him.

"YOU'RE VERY LOVELY FOR A HUMAN." THE VAMPIRE stroked Abigail's arm as the carriage swayed.

"Thank you," Abigail said.

"My name is Joven." The vampire traced his hand along her collarbone, and she crossed her arms over her naked breasts and huddled more deeply against the velvet cushion of the carriage.

"You're going to make a wonderful pet. I can tell." Joven smiled at her and she swallowed thickly.

"What's your name, human?"

"Abigail."

He frowned. "I do not like that name. From now on you will be known as Jarah. Joven and Jarah – doesn't that go together nicely?"

She nodded and flinched back when he traced the flesh of her arm. "Tell me, Jarah, have you been bitten before?"

Abigail took a deep breath and stared at her tightly folded arms. "Yes."

"Did you find it pleasing?"

"No."

"That's a shame. I think you will find my touch to be very enjoyable."

"Please, could I have a shirt?"

Joven grinned at her. "And hide those magnificent breasts? I think not. I like my pets to wear as little clothing as possible."

Abigail bit her lip and stared out the window of the carriage into the darkness. "Are we going to your home?"

Joven shook his head as he continued to stroke Abigail's arm. "No. We are on our way to the home of a very powerful vampire. I have business with him."

"What kind of business?"

A look of irritation crossed Joven's face and he squeezed her arm until she gasped with pain. "Do not ask me my business. Do you understand, pet?"

She nodded, a look of fear crossing her face. He relaxed and smiled at her. "You know, I wasn't planning on stopping at that hovel of an establishment, but I was tired and thirsty and it was the only place for miles where a vampire could get a drink. I'm so glad I stopped. I would have missed out on the opportunity to purchase you if I hadn't. When I saw you on that stage I thought you would make a fine gift for my new business partner. But now, I fear I must keep you for my own. A vampire would have to be a fool to give up such a magnificent creature."

Joven moved closer to her on the seat and put his arm around her shoulders. "I am still thirsty, my pet."

"Please, don't do this," she whispered.

He laughed. "I promise I will make it painless. In fact, if you are a good girl and please me well, I will make sure -"

The carriage bumped to a stop. There was a muffled thud from outside and Joven frowned. He stood and reached for the door. As he opened it, he looked behind him at Abby. "Stay where you are, pet. Do not -"

He jerked and a look of surprise flickered across his face. He looked down at the sword embedded deep in his chest before staring at the man in the hooded cloak standing on the steps of the carriage.

"What?" He whispered.

Abigail cried out as Joven exploded into ash. Her eyes widened with shock when the man pushed the hood back and revealed his face.

"Hello, little dove."

———

"What have you done?" Abigail cried. She stood and shoved Val in the chest. Not expecting it, he stumbled and fell off the steps, landing on the hard ground with a thud.

Abigail shot down the steps toward him. Hard hands came out of the darkness and grabbed her. A tall and lean vampire with blond hair and blue eyes, pulled her into his embrace.

"Hello, pretty one." He grinned at her. "I'm not sure what it is about you that has Val so hot and bothered but I for one, am anxious to find out." He dipped his head toward her throat and stopped when he felt the blade against his chest.

"Any closer and I'll use your own blade to send you to hell. Do you understand, leech?" Abigail said.

Faren blinked in surprise and released her. She showed him the dagger from his belt and he held his hands up as she backed away, his dagger clenched tightly in her hand.

"Easy, my pet." He smiled at her.

"I am not your pet," she said. She retreated until her back hit the carriage. A flicker of purple caught her eye and she inhaled when the small pixie hovered anxiously in front of her.

A small smile crossed her face. "Hello, little one."

Violet zoomed forward with her entire body glowing brightly, and planted kisses across Abigail's cheeks and forehead.

Abigail laughed. "Okay, okay. I'm happy to see you too, Violet."

As Violet landed on her shoulder, Abigail looked down at Val. He had moved into a sitting position and was staring silently at her.

"You shouldn't have done that, Val."

He scowled and rose gracefully to his feet. "I shouldn't have saved your life?"

He moved towards her and she held the dagger up warningly. "Don't come any closer."

"Don't come any closer? I have searched for you for months, Abigail. Now that I have found you, I cannot touch you?"

She didn't reply, and he held his hand out to her. "Put the dagger down, little dove. Come to me."

She shook her head as there was a rustling in the trees behind them. Val whirled around and raised his sword as three men stepped out of the trees. They all carried swords and they stared unblinkingly at Val and Faren.

"Abigail? Have you been hurt?" The biggest of them, a dark-skinned man with brown eyes and a bald head, called out.

"I'm fine, Wesley. I – I know him," Abigail replied. "Put your swords away."

When neither the three men nor Val moved, she cursed under her breath. "Put them away I said. Val, these men are my friends."

After a moment, Val sheathed his sword and the three men did the same. They approached the carriage, staring warily at Faren and Val.

"Where is Joven?" Wesley asked.

"He's dead."

"Bloody hell!" A red-headed man, his skin fair and covered in freckles, spit on the ground. "What the fuck, Abby! You weren't supposed to kill him!"

"I didn't, Evan!" She protested. "Everything was going according to plan and then these two showed up."

"What do we do now?" The third man, he was white-haired and missing his left eye, asked.

"We're screwed," Evan said. "We needed Joven to get in and now he's dead. We'll never find a way in now."

"Shut up, Evan," Wesley said. "We'll find another way."

He approached Abby, his eyes dropping to her naked breasts. Val growled warningly. Wesley ignored him and stripped off his shirt, handing it to Abby. She pulled it over her head and gave him a smile of thanks. She ignored the jealous look Val gave the both of them.

"We need to get this carriage off the road before someone sees it," Wesley said. "Where is the driver?"

Faren, leaning against the carriage, studied his fingernails. "I was thirsty."

He pointed to the side of the road where the driver's crumpled body could be seen. "I'm afraid I may have drunk a little too much."

"I told you not to kill the human, Faren," Val said.

Faren shrugged. "You're not the boss of me. I agreed to help you at the risk of my own life. Why should I not take my reward?"

Moving with a silent speed that Val had never suspected in her, Abigail stood in front of Faren and held the dagger to his chest. "If you so much as look at me or any of my friends, I will gut you like a fish and rip your heart out with your own dagger. Do you understand me?"

"Oh, I like her." Faren grinned at Val. "I can see why you wanted to go after her."

He gave a squeal of shock and pain when Abby shoved the dagger into his breastbone. "I am inches away from your heart, leech," she whispered. "One little push and you'll be nothing more than a pile of ash. You do not touch any of us. Do I make myself clear?"

"Perfectly," Faren said.

She yanked the dagger from his chest, ignoring his wince of pain and the steady stream of blood that began to flow from his wound. "They come with us."

"Are you crazy?" Evan said. "They'll kill us while we sleep."

"No, they won't," Abigail replied. "Besides, we're going to need them."

She reached up and stroked Violet's thin leg. The pixie grinned happily before kissing her neck.

"What the hell happened to you, Abigail?" Val said.

She stared grimly at him. "I stopped being afraid."

VAL STARED AT ABIGAIL FROM ACROSS THE CAMPFIRE. THE three humans had carefully manoeuvered the carriage into the trees until they became too thick for the bulky carriage to go any further. Evan and the older man, Bill, had disappeared and returned with three horses. Abigail had used the carriage to change and Val couldn't stop staring at her. She was wearing a plain short sleeved shirt with a leather vest over it and tight, dark cotton pants. Knee-high leather boots completed the outfit. The pants clung to her ass and he could feel his cock stirring in his pants at the sight of her lush curves. A short, curved sword hung around her waist, a knife was strapped around her right thigh and he could see the handle of a dagger sticking out of the top of her boot. Wide silver cuffs were around her wrists and a band of silver around her throat.

He couldn't believe the difference in her. It wasn't just the weight loss; it was in the way she moved and the way she spoke. The Abigail he had known before had been a frightened little mouse. This Abigail had an aura of confidence and strength that he hadn't known existed inside of her.

He was desperate to take her away from Faren and the others. He could barely stop himself from touching her, but when he had tried to sit down beside her she had given him a warning look and immediately moved to the opposite side of the fire. She had sat down on the fallen log next to Wesley, smiling fondly at him. Val had to tamp down his urge to kill the man.

"So, this is cozy." Faren grinned at the group before checking the wound on his chest. It was nearly healed, and he gave a grunt of satisfaction before peering at Val who was still staring at Abigail.

"You two obviously know each other," he said to Abigail. "Are you the reason Val is so soft-hearted towards the humans?"

Abigail, who was stroking Violet's back as the little pixie perched on her knee, didn't reply.

Val cleared his throat. "Tell me what happened, Abigail."

Even from across the fire he could see the way that Violet glowed with happiness. The bug hadn't gone near him since the moment she had flown to Abby, and he ignored the trickle of hurt. He was being ridiculous.

"Tell me," he prompted.

Abigail sighed. "The vampire that took me carried me to – I don't really know where – some section of the forest. I have no idea how far he carried me. It happened so fast."

She continued to stroke Violet's back, staring down at the small pixie. "I got lucky. A man named Michael was hunting in the forest. He literally stumbled onto us and killed the vampire before he could feed from me.

"A human killed a vampire that easily?" Faren frowned.

Evan snorted. "It happens all the time, leech."

"Obviously he was distracted by his hunger," Faren retorted.

Evan started to protest, and Abby shook her head at him. He lapsed into silence and stared moodily at the small campfire.

"Michael took me back to his people and I've been with them ever since."

"That's it?" Val said.

"Yes."

He gave her an angry look. "You're not the same, Abigail."

She shrugged. "Michael is very skilled at killing vampires. He's been teaching others how to kill them and when I asked him to teach me, he agreed. I've spent the last year training with him. He taught me how to find their weaknesses and how to – to not be afraid anymore."

"How did you get captured for the auction?" Faren asked.

"I allowed myself to be captured." Abigail gave him a look of contempt. "Michael has been taken by a vampire named Darius."

Faren started and Abigail raised her eyebrow at him. "You know him?"

"I know of him," Faren corrected. He glanced at Val. "There are some ugly rumours about him."

"They are not rumours," Bill said.

"What are you talking about?" Val asked.

"This vampire, this Darius, has been taking humans and keeping them prisoner in his estate. He's waged war against the humans," Abigail replied.

Faren rolled his eyes. "That's a bit of an exaggeration."

"Bullshit!" Wesley snapped. "Your kind has been using us like cattle for years. This world would be a much better place if the vampire plague had wiped all of you from the face of the earth."

"What is he doing with the humans?" Val asked, ignoring Wesley's outburst.

"He's been using them for his own sick little games. He pits them against each other in death battles, and invites other vampires to watch and make bets as to who will win. It's become quite popular and apparently there's quite the wait list to watch the games. Vampires either pay money to watch the games or they provide Darius with new humans to fight in the games."

"Why did you allow yourself to be auctioned?"

Abigail glanced at Wesley. "Darius had invited Joven to his estate. Joven has his own large estate and Darius is anxious to expand. He wants Joven to join him in his little business venture. He would hold games at his estate in the west and Joven would hold games at his estate in the east. Darius would take a generous cut of the proceeds of course."

Val frowned. "Why did Joven not just start his own games? Why does he need Darius' permission?"

"Darius has killed any other leeches who have tried to mimic the games."

"I told you – that's nothing but ugly rumours," Faren said.

"No, it isn't," Abigail replied.

"Anyway," she took a deep breath, "we found out that Joven was meeting with Darius to discuss their new business arrangement. We have been following Joven for days and when we realized he was stopping at the auction house, I allowed myself to be captured in the hopes that Joven would purchase me. Darius' estate is heavily guarded, and we needed a way to get in."

Val stared at her in disbelief. "So, you put yourself in harm's way? How did you know that Joven would even purchase you? What if another had purchased you? What would you have done then? Did you think of that, Abigail?"

His voice was rising and he could feel anger burning in his belly. If he hadn't stopped at the auction house tonight, Joven would be feeding from Abigail at this very moment.

Abigail gave him a cool look. "We've been watching Joven for a long time, Val. He has a certain taste and I fit the bill. We were quite certain that he would purchase me."

Val snorted angrily. "If I hadn't killed him when I did, he'd be feeding from you right now. You know that."

She shrugged. "I will do whatever it takes to save Michael."

"Have you gone mad?" Val asked. "Is that it?"

"No. I told you - Michael saved my life and I owe him a debt. I pay my debts in full."

"I remember," he said.

"It doesn't matter," Evan said. "Thanks to that goddamn leech, Joven is dead. We've lost our chance to save Michael."

"Maybe not." Abigail said.

Evan glanced at her. "What do you mean?"

"Darius and Joven have never met in person. All we need is a vampire to pose as Joven." She stared at Val and he shook his head.

"I will not."

"You have to." Abigail glared at him, her hand clenching into a tight fist. "This is your fault, Val, and you're going to help us get into Darius' estate."

"No," Val said.

Abigail took a deep breath and looked at Faren. He held up his hands. "No way, pet. You can count me out of your little suicide mission."

"Coward!" She snarled and turned back to Val.

"I won't put you in deliberate danger, little dove. Do not ask me to do so."

"Neil and Maria are in there," she said.

Val jerked in surprise. "How do you know that?"

"We have someone in the estate already," Wesley said. "He's been sending us information."

"Then use him to get past the guards," Val said. "Why do you need Abigail?"

"It would be too dangerous for him. There is no way he can get us into the estate without his betrayal being discovered. He'll be killed," Abigail replied.

"This is madness, Abigail!" Val suddenly shouted. "You're playing a game you can't possibly win. I will not allow you to do this."

"Allow me?" Abigail stood, ignoring Violet's frown as she tumbled from her knee, and marched around the fire. She stood in front of Val and glared at him.

"You have no right to tell me what to do. I do what I want."

He stood and scowled at her. "Have you forgotten what happened between us?"

"Shut up!" She glanced at the others.

Val arched his eyebrow. "Do they not know, little dove? Do they not know that you belong - "

"I said, shut up!" She punched him hard in the stomach. He flinched but grabbed her arm and yanked her against him before she could move away.

Her three companions stood and drew their swords. Val paid no attention to them. It was the first time he had touched Abigail in thirteen months, and the feel of her body against his was intoxicating.

"Let her go, leech," Wesley said.

Abigail held up her hand as Val put his arm around her waist and stroked her hip through her pants. "Just wait, Wesley."

She bit her lip. "Val, I'm asking you to help us. Help Maria and Neil – they're your friends, remember? Please, we can't do this without you."

He stared into her dark brown eyes. "I will help you, but I want something in return."

She stiffened and tried to pull away, but he wouldn't let her go. "I won't let you feed from me, Val."

He smiled and brushed his thumb across her lower lip. "That is not what I want, little dove."

He let his eyes drift down her body and when he glanced up at her face, he was thrilled to see the hot blush in her cheeks.

"So, you do remember," he murmured.

"Val -"

"Make your decision, Abigail. I will help you break into this Darius' home if you spend the night with me."

"What?" Wesley shouted. "No! Abby, we will find another way. I'm not letting this leech touch you!"

Val gave Wesley a smug grin. "It is not your decision to make, human. Do we have an agreement, little dove?"

She hesitated only briefly before nodding and Wesley cursed vehemently.

"He'll bite you, Abigail. You know he will."

"He won't," Abigail replied. "Do I have your word that you won't, Val?"

Val smiled at her. "Yes." A predatory grin crossed his face. "I will not bite you until you ask me to bite you."

"I won't ask you." She flushed at his knowing smile.

"Of course you won't."

She glanced at Faren. "And him? I want his word that he'll stay away from the others."

Faren held his hands up innocently and gave her a charming smile that she didn't return.

"If you touch any of them, Faren, I'll kill you. I'll hunt you down and rip out your heart. Do you understand?" Val said.

Faren gave him a mock look of hurt. "I thought we were friends, Val."

"Do you understand that I will kill you?"

Faren saluted him. "Perfectly, my friend. I give you my word that I won't touch your human friends. Besides, I'm still full of driver blood."

Val took Abigail's hand and Wesley stepped forward. Val arched his eyebrow at him. "I don't need your assistance for this, human."

Wesley's hands clenched into fists and he grunted with anger. Abigail gave him a pleading look. "It is the only way, Wesley."

"No, it isn't, Abigail."

"Yes, it is." She replied as Val led her toward the carriage.

CHAPTER 3

Abigail took a deep breath and tried to calm the butterflies in her stomach. From the moment Val had pushed back his hood, she'd had to restrain herself from throwing her arms around him. Lust and need had enveloped her like a thick cloud, and she was angry and disgusted with herself. She had spent the last year convincing herself that it had been his bite that had made her feel what she did and to have it so immediately obvious that it wasn't, angered and confused her.

She felt like everything she had worked so hard for over the last year had been swept away the moment she laid eyes on Val. She was still anxious to save Michael and Neil and Maria, but the anxiety was buried under a wave of need for Val that was so strong it took her breath away.

She had never considered herself much of an actress, but she thought she'd done a remarkable acting job in the last half hour. It was a sheer battle to keep her true feelings hidden from both Val and the others. When Val had put his arm around her waist and stared at her body, the familiar hunger for him had coursed through her veins and she had damn near leaned in and kissed him.

When he had given her his terms for helping her, she had made herself hesitate before agreeing. There was no way in hell she was letting him know how much she wanted him and how eager she was to fuck him again. She was baffled and more than a little embarrassed by her body's response to him.

She took another deep breath as Val opened the door to the carriage. She would hide how good it felt when he touched her and, no matter what happened, she would not beg him to bite her. She had vowed never to be a goddamn meal ticket for a vampire again. While she might fuck Val and love every minute of it, she wouldn't break that vow.

"Go on, bug," Val said when Violet landed on her shoulder.

Violet frowned at him and clung to Abby's hair.

"It's okay, little one. Go and stay with Wesley. He won't harm you, I promise," Abby said.

Violet pouted, and Abby smiled a little. "I will spend all day with you tomorrow, my sweet Violet. Go on now."

With a small frown, Violet flew to Wesley. She landed on his broad shoulder and stared up at him for a moment. He ignored her and gave Abigail a look of hurt and betrayal. She bit her lip and gave him a wavering smile that he didn't return.

Joven's carriage was large with seats long enough for a person to stretch out on. She examined the shutters on the inside of the carriage windows carefully. It was obvious that Joven used this as a sleeping compartment as well, and the shutters were made of thick wood and impenetrable by sunlight.

Val latched and locked the door of the carriage before sitting back on the seat. He smiled at her as she sat on the edge of the seat on the opposite side of the carriage and wrapped her arms around herself.

"I've looked for you for many months, little dove."

"Well, now you've found me."

"I've missed you."

She cleared her throat but didn't respond and he frowned at her. "Are you fucking the human?"

"Which human?"

"The dark-skinned one."

"He has a name. It's Wesley."

"Are you fucking Wesley?" He asked.

"That's none of your business."

"You will tell me what I want to know," he said through gritted teeth.

"Talking wasn't part of the deal. We're in this carriage for one thing and I'd appreciate it if we could just get it over with."

"Just get it over with?" For a moment, it looked like hurt flashed across his face. "Is that what you really want? To get this over with?"

She didn't reply. Instead, she removed her various weapons. He watched as she pulled the dagger from her boot and unbuckled both the knife from around her thigh and the sword around her waist.

"Do you know how to use those?"

"Yes."

"Perhaps we should put them outside of the carriage for the night then." He grinned at her but she shook her head.

"They stay within my reaching distance, Val."

"You no longer trust me, little dove? No longer accept that you belong to me, and I will keep you safe?"

She laughed and pulled off her boots. "I've spent the last year taking care of myself, learning to kill your kind and being fairly successful at it. So, no – I don't need you to keep me safe."

"But you still belong to me," he said.

"No. I do not."

He was sitting beside her before she could blink, his large hand wrapped in her braid and his breath warm on her face. "You will always belong to me. Always!"

"No, I -"

He kissed her, his tongue thrusting between her lips, and she reminded herself to not show him her need before she was throwing her arms around him and kissing him back with wild abandonment.

Val hissed in pain when she cupped his face. She pulled away, her eyes wide with guilt.

"I'm sorry. I forgot."

The bands of silver around her wrists had touched his neck and his skin was burning. She slipped the bands off and dropped them into her boots, giving him another guilty look. "I'm sorry."

"Around your neck as well." He pointed to the band that hugged her neck and she unclipped it and added it to the wrist bands.

She examined his neck. "Are you all right?"

"Yes." He sat back on the seat. "Straddle me."

She swallowed nervously and then swung her leg over his lap. She sat on his knees and he grabbed her ass, pulling her forward until her crotch was pressing against his erection.

She made a soft moan of need and he tugged on the back of her neck. "Kiss me."

She leaned down and he quickly unbraided her hair as she kissed him with soft brushes of her lips against his. Her long hair fell around them like a dark curtain, and he stroked it as he pushed his tongue into her mouth.

She sucked on his tongue, pulling a groan from his throat, and he slid his hands under her shirt. He hissed again, yanking his hands out from under the fabric and staring at the burns on the tips of his fingers.

"Shit!" She gave him a look of embarrassment and quickly stripped off her shirt. She was wearing a very thin, white undershirt underneath it and his eyes narrowed at the sight of her nipples poking against the material.

She unwound the silver chain draped around her waist. "Sorry."

He gently pushed her off his lap. "Do you have any other hidden silver, little dove?"

"Um, yeah. On my legs."

"Show me." He indicated for her to take her pants off and she stood up. Feeling oddly embarrassed, she started to shimmy out of her pants.

"Slowly," he instructed.

She bit her bottom lip, her flush deepening, but did what he asked. She slowly skimmed her pants down to reveal the wide band of silver wrapped around each pale thigh and the cuff of silver around each calf.

"Very clever," he said. "Take them off."

She added them to the growing pile of silver in her boots and was about to sit down beside him when he shook his head. "No, stand in front of me, Abigail."

She stood in the middle of the carriage, her arms crossed over her breasts, and her pulse thudding so loudly she knew he would easily hear it. He stared silently at her until she gave him an irritated look.

"If you've changed your mind about fucking me, Val, just say the word. I'll be happy to go back to my friends."

He stood in front of her. "Undress me."

She scowled at him. "Are your arms broken? Undress yourself."

He leaned in and brushed his lips across her throbbing pulse. "Undress me, Abigail."

She swallowed thickly and unbuttoned his cloak from around his throat. She folded it neatly and set it on the seat behind her before reaching for his shirt. He raised his arms and she tugged it off his body. She inhaled, the beat of her pulse increasing when his pale torso was revealed. A smug smile crossed his face.

She ignored it and reached for the button on his pants. He put his hand over hers. "Not yet. Take this off." He tugged on the hem of her undershirt.

She sighed with frustration and reached for the shirt.

"Slowly," he reminded her. She eased it over her head. Before she could pull it free of her arms, he had bent and sucked her right nipple into his mouth. She gave a surprised cry, her back arching as his lips pulled hard on her nipple, and struggled to free her arms of the undershirt.

She gripped his head in her hands as his hand came up to knead and cup her other breast. His fingers pinched her nipple and she jerked against him. "Val!"

He pulled away, breathing harshly and holding her away when she tried to press herself up against him. "My pants. Take them off me."

He kicked his boots off as she fumbled with the button to his pants. She yanked them down his legs. Every nerve in her body was screaming to be touched by him, and she moaned when his hard cock was revealed.

She crouched down to help him step out of his pants. She tossed them behind her and wasn't at all surprised when she felt his hand on the top of her head. He pushed her into a kneeling position in front of him. His cock was only inches from her mouth, and she couldn't stop herself from licking her lips at the sight of it.

"Like I taught you, little dove," he said.

Once he had discovered how naïve she was about sex, Val had spent an entire night teaching her how to please him with her mouth. She was nervous at first, but he had been patient with her. His loud groans and the continuous string of compliments flowing from his mouth as she had sucked and licked him, had made wetness drip down her thighs.

She licked her lips again, this time with nervousness. She shook her head at herself when she realized she was worried he wouldn't find her pleasing anymore. She had lost more than seventy pounds, and she had found her courage. If he had found her attractive when she was a fat, scared mouse – he would find her attractive now.

Of course he finds you attractive, idiot. His giant erection is a pretty big indication that he finds your new body hot. The real question is – why do you care if you please him? You're doing this only to gain his help to save Michael. After tonight, you can't have sex with him again. It's too much of a distraction.

"Abigail," Val prompted. His hand tightened in her hair and he drew her mouth toward his cock. She opened her mouth wide and took his cock deep into her mouth. He groaned and his hips thrust forward as she licked the under-side of his cock with her warm tongue. She held the base of his cock in her hand and squeezed as she bobbed her head back and forth over his large cock.

He groaned again and threaded both hands through her hair. He held her head still as he pushed his cock back and forth in her mouth.

"I love watching you suck my cock, little dove," he whispered. "I love how your lips look sliding back and forth over it."

She moaned, and he inhaled when her lips vibrated around his hard shaft.

"Good girl." He moaned and pushed his cock to the back of her throat. She fought her gag reflex and licked and sucked firmly on his cock as she stroked the base of it with her fingers.

He pulled his cock free and stared down at her. "Have you done this to the human? Has he felt your mouth on his cock?"

"That's none of your business," she whispered.

He stared at her swollen mouth. A fleeting look of anger crossing his face before he stroked her hair back from her face. "Tell me."

"I'm not telling you anything."

He pulled her to her feet and yanked her panties down to her ankles. She stepped out of them and he stared at the dark curls between her thighs with a look of terrible hunger.

"Val?" She whispered. He tore his gaze away and kissed her until she was breathless and clinging weakly to him. He sat down on the seat of the carriage, pulling on her waist until she straddled his lap.

He rubbed his fingers across her soaking wet clit. She cried out, her hips arching, and he gave a small smile of satisfaction.

"You've missed fucking me."

She shook her head. "No, I -"

He guided his cock into her wet pussy, pushing just the head of it into her. He stopped her when she tried to grind herself against him.

"Tell me the truth, little dove. You've missed my cock, haven't you?" He tugged her head down and licked and sucked on her earlobe. "I want to hear you say it."

"Val, please," she moaned.

"Say it," he demanded.

"I've missed fucking you. I've missed your cock," she whispered.

"I've missed you too," he breathed and thrust his cock fully into her.

She cried out, her fingers digging into his shoulders as they rocked and thrust against each other. He rubbed her clit, bringing her closer and closer to orgasm. She moaned and gasped and then kissed him hard, shoving her tongue deep into his mouth. He held her tightly around the waist and slammed his cock in and out of her.

Abigail moaned repeatedly as Val's hard cock rubbed against her wet walls. The combination of his thick cock and his rough fingers against her clit had her burning with desire. She could feel her orgasm starting to flow through her and she cried out and hammered her fists against his chest when he stopped touching her. He pushed her back, withdrawing until just the head of his cock was inside of her.

"Val! Don't stop!"

Val gripped the back of her neck. "Are you fucking the human?"

"What?" She cried. "Val, have you gone mad?"

"Has he taken what belongs to me? Has he touched what only I am allowed to touch?" He asked in a low, strained voice.

She growled with anger and leaned down. "Fuck me!" She nearly shouted and bit his bottom lip with a fierceness that surprised him.

Unable to take the torment any longer, he thrust deep and she cried out with pleasure and shock. His hands moved to her hips, and he plunged into her twice more before she stiffened and her back arched. She cried out his name, her entire body shuddering and her pussy tightening around his throbbing cock.

"Abigail!" He shouted and came violently inside of her. His fangs lengthened, and he dipped his head to her shoulder.

At the feel of his teeth against her, she jerked and wound her hands into his hair, yanking his head back.

"Don't! You promised."

VAL SHUDDERED ALL OVER. ABIGAIL'S REFUSAL TO LET HIM feed had rocked him to his core. He made a low moan of need and found himself begging for the first time in his life. "Please, little dove. Please."

"No," she whispered as her body continued to shudder around him.

He bit his own lip until it bled, and she made a soft sound of distress. "Stop, Val. Don't do that."

He turned his head away as the last of his climax rushed through him and she stroked his hair. He leaned back and stared blankly at the side of the carriage. The need to bite and feed from Abigail was overwhelming him, and he was dangerously close to throwing her to the floor and sinking his fangs into her soft skin.

He drew in a deep breath, his hands clenched into tight fists.

"Val?" She whispered. He twitched when her fingers traced his jaw.

"Get off me, Abigail."

She pushed away from him and huddled on the seat opposite him. Without looking at her, he said, "Go back to your friends."

"I thought – I thought you wanted me to spend the night with you."

He shook his head. "No, I want you to leave."

She hurriedly put on her clothes, her face bright red and tears gathering on her lashes. She grabbed her boots and her weapons. "Are you – will you keep your promise to help us?"

"Yes," he said.

"Val, what -"

From the corner of his eye he could see her reaching for him and he flinched away.

"Get out, Abigail! I've taken what I wanted from you – now leave!" He shouted harshly.

She made a soft sound of hurt and stumbled out of the carriage, slamming the door shut behind her.

CHAPTER 4

"Abigail, are you sure you're okay?"

"I'm fine, Wesley. Stop worrying." She made herself smile at him as he sat down next to her.

Violet, her face creased with anxiety, was sitting on her shoulder stroking her cheek repeatedly and Wesley smiled a little.

"I've never seen a pixie so attached to a human before."

"Violet's different." Abigail turned and kissed the top of the pixie's head

"Will you tell me what happened?" Wesley asked.

"You know what happened." She stared steadily at him and he flushed and looked away.

"I'll kill him for what he did to you."

"Stop it, Wesley. He didn't hurt me."

She stared into the fire, barely feeling Violet's soft hand stroking her cheek. Val had come out of the carriage ten minutes after she did. Without looking at any of them, he disappeared into the woods. Faren stretched lazily, nodded to the humans, and followed him. That had been hours ago, and they hadn't seen either vampire since.

At Wesley's urging, Abigail had crawled into some blankets next to the fire and tried to sleep. It was impossible. She had lain quietly for a few hours before getting up for her shift on watch.

Now, she stared at Evan and Bill's sleeping forms and rubbed at her temples. She told Val she would not ask him to bite her, but she was surprised at how strong the urge was to give in to his need. She wanted him to bite her, wanted to feel his teeth sinking into her flesh as her orgasm rushed through her.

He believed that she would give in to her urge to be bitten by him, and he was hurt and upset that she wouldn't let him. Still, she hadn't expected such an extreme reaction from him and she was confused by it.

She cursed herself in her head. Val was a vampire, not a human. While he had an obvious sexual need for her, she was a fool if she thought that's all it was. He would always want to bite her, to drink his fill of her blood, and for that reason alone it would never work between them.

Why not? He fed from you before and you enjoyed it, remember?

That may have been true, but she had been weak and afraid then. She was different now. She didn't need to give Val her blood in exchange for his protection. She could take care of herself.

You're fooling yourself if you believe his protection was the only reason you let him feed from you.

She shut out the voice in her head and forced herself to pay attention to Wesley.

"We need to come up with a new plan for getting into Darius' home."

She frowned. "Why?"

Wesley gave her an impatient look. "Because your vampire friend isn't coming back, Abby."

"Yes, he is."

Wesley sighed. "No, he isn't." He glanced at the lightening sky. "It's almost dawn. He won't be back."

"He will be," she insisted. "He promised to help us, and he will. Trust me, Wesley."

"How do you even know him?" Wesley asked.

"He was with the group of humans who found me when I was pulled from my world to this one. I was attacked by vampires and Val saved my life. He was injured with silver and was dying. I allowed him to feed from me."

"You what?" Wesley shouted. She made a hushing motion. Evan snorted in his sleep and burrowed deeper into his blankets.

"He saved my life. I owed him a debt."

"Are you crazy, Abby? What's the first rule Michael taught us? Never let them bite you. You know what it does to a human."

"Yes, I do," she said.

He was giving her a look bordering on contempt and her patience snapped. "Judge me all you want, Wesley, but Val isn't like other vampires. He's saved more human lives than you can imagine. He's good."

"There are no good vampires, Abby."

She gave him an angry look. "You know that's not true."

"Jaxen is different," Wesley replied.

"So is Val."

"No, he isn't. Val saved your life so he could fuck you and feed from you," Wesley grunted.

He stared at her exposed neck. "Did you ask him to bite you tonight where it would not show?"

"Fuck you, Wesley! I told you I wouldn't let him bite me

and I didn't. You can believe me or not. I don't care either way."

He stared angrily at her and then sighed. "I'm sorry, Abby. I just - "

He stopped as Faren, followed by Val, strolled into the camp. Her body vibrating excitedly, Violet flew from Abby's shoulder to Val's. She tangled herself in his hair and kissed his neck affectionately.

"Hello, bug." He reached into his pocket and pulled out a small piece of dried meat. He handed it to her and she kissed his neck again before chewing at it.

Abby stood up nervously. "Val, are - "

Ignoring her, he walked to the carriage and opened the door. He whispered something to Violet and she nodded before flying back to Abigail.

"Are you going or not, Faren?" He asked.

Faren shrugged. "Why not. At the very least, there will be plenty of humans at Darius' home to feed from." He winked at Abigail and Wesley and followed Val into the carriage. They shut the door behind them as the sun peeked over the horizon.

Abby swallowed down the hurt she felt at Val's refusal to acknowledge her and smiled at Wesley. "Let's wake the others and pack up. It's at least three days to Darius' home. We should get going."

———

VAL FOLLOWED FAREN FROM THE CARRIAGE. THE SUN HAD set but it was still light enough for him to see that Abigail was missing.

Faren glanced around the woods with dismay. "What the hell? You couldn't have stopped in a town?"

Wesley frowned at him. "We thought it best if we kept a low profile."

"Your low profile doesn't keep me fed," Faren said. He eyed Evan with interest and the redhead stiffened and drew his sword.

"Enough, Faren," Val said. "Remember what I told you."

"Yes, yes, you'll kill me if I touch the humans." Faren waved his hand irritably at him. "But you cannot expect me to feed from wildlife every night like you do."

"Go and find a town or a village. There's bound to be one fairly close," Val said. "I'm sure with your good looks and charm, you'll have no trouble finding a human to feed from."

Wesley made a snort of disgust that Faren ignored. "Are you coming with me?"

Val shook his head and Faren rolled his eyes before turning to the humans. "Good night gentlemen. I'll see you in the morning."

He disappeared in a blur of movement and Val turned to the bald human.

"Where is Abigail?"

"Why?" Wesley asked.

He gave a strangled gasp as Val sped across the camp and grabbed him by the throat. He lifted the large man a few inches from the ground and shook him roughly before dropping him to the ground and kneeling on his broad chest.

Without looking behind him, he said, "Kill me, redhead, and you'll never get into Darius' estate."

Evan hesitated, and Wesley gave him a grim nod. He lowered his sword and took a few steps back as Val stared at Wesley.

"You should know that I killed the last human who dared to touch her. If you wish to keep your head firmly attached to your body, it would be wise of you to keep your distance from her."

"I'm her friend." Wesley glared at him.

"Her friend? Or her lover?"

He refused to answer, and Val hissed in anger. "He was her friend as well. I did not care for the way he looked at her."

He leaned even closer, his eyes glowing. "You look at her the same way."

"Get off me," Wesley snapped.

"Tell me where Abigail is." Val held his hand up and Wesley watched as his fingernails lengthened into sharp points. He traced one across Wesley's throat, smiling when the big man inhaled sharply.

"Tell me, *Wesley*." Val grinned at him.

"There's a lake to the north. She and the pixie went to get water."

"You let her go alone?" Anger crossed Val's face. For one bleak moment, Wesley was certain the vampire would kill him.

"She can take care of herself." Bill spoke up.

"Can she, old man?" Val glared at him.

"She's better with the sword than all three of us," he said nervously. "Besides, it is only a short distance away."

Val turned back to Wesley. "If I see you touching her, I'll kill you. Do we have an understanding?"

"Yes," Wesley bit out.

"Good." Val patted him lightly on the cheek and disappeared into the woods before Wesley could blink.

"Jesus." Bill wiped a shaking hand across his forehead. "He's going to kill us all, Wesley. We should kill him first."

Wesley shook his head. "We need him. He's our best shot for rescuing Michael. Besides, he won't kill us."

40

"Are you sure about that?" Evan asked.

"No."

———

"THERE, DOESN'T THAT FEEL BETTER?"

Val stood at the edge of the tree line and watched as Abigail, sitting on a large rock that jutted out over the water, dumped a small cup of water over Violet. The little pixie was naked and soap was sluicing down her skin. Abby, wearing a towel and her skin and dark hair damp with moisture, scooped more water out of the lake and poured it over her.

"Honestly, Violet, I don't think you've bathed since I last saw you," Abby teased.

Violet grinned at her and flew into the air above her. She twirled, spinning faster and faster until her wings and body were a blur. Tiny droplets of water mixed with pixie dust sprinkled on to Abby and she smiled fondly at the pixie.

Violet abruptly stopped spinning and dropped onto Abby's thigh. Her formerly wet purple hair was now dry, and it surrounded her head in a huge wind-blown halo.

Val smiled a little as Abby giggled. "Now that gives a whole new meaning to air dry."

Violet patted her hair and preened prettily before turning and wiggling her naked ass at her. Abby laughed again.

"You have no shame, little one." She handed Violet her dress and then suddenly whipped around, her hand reaching for something on the rock beside her. Val had moved up behind her and he blinked as he felt the dagger at her throat.

"Careful, Abigail." He was impressed by her quickness. He thought he'd been completely silent and yet she had still heard him.

"Don't sneak up on me like that!" She snapped at him as she pulled the dagger back. "I could have killed you."

"Doubtful." His gaze moved down her damp body. "Your towel is slipping."

She glanced down, a hot blush rising to her face, when she realized her towel had slipped down to the top of her noticeably erect nipples. She yanked the towel up and slid off the rock. Her clothes were lying on the ground and she picked them up, glancing back at Val.

"Turn around."

"Don't you think it's a little late for modesty, Abigail?"

"Just turn around, please." She replied.

He turned and stared at the lake. Her wings whirring, Violet hovered in front of him. She preened for him, turning to the left and the right and fluttering her eyelashes at him.

He grinned in spite of himself. "Yes, bug, you look very pretty. And you smell much better as well."

She scowled at him and zoomed forward. He waited for her nip, the little bug had a habit of biting when she was displeased, but she only kissed him on the nose before hovering in front of him again.

"You're in a good mood." He raised his eyebrow at her, and she shrugged and darted past his shoulder.

"I'm done," Abigail said.

He turned and stared her up and down. She was strapping her knife around her pant-clad thigh and she smiled when Violet pulled playfully on her damp hair.

"What I wouldn't give for a hair dryer."

"A what?" Val asked.

"A hair dryer. It was a type of – of machine that ran on electricity. You plugged it into an outlet in the wall of your home and used it to dry your hair."

"Electricity?"

She sighed. "Never mind."

She began to braid her hair as Violet landed on her shoulder.

"Thank you for taking care of Violet. I was worried about her. I'm glad that she had you to look after her."

He shrugged. "I tried to get rid of her. The bug refused to leave."

Violet stuck her tongue out at him, and Abigail snorted softly. "I doubt that's true."

She finished braiding her hair and tied the end with a thin piece of leather before picking up two large wooden buckets. She dipped them into the lake and carried them through the trees. Val took them from her, and she gave him a nod of thanks.

"From now on, you're not to go anywhere without me. Do you understand?" He said as they picked their way through the trees.

"I can take care of myself."

"Just do as I say, Abigail."

She shook her head. "No. You don't get to tell me what to do."

"Abigail -"

"Drop it, Val. A lot has changed in the last year. I'm not the person I was before, and I don't need yours or anyone else's protection."

He grunted in reply and she gave him a quick look. "Thank you for helping us."

"It's not going to work."

She frowned. "What do you mean?"

"Abigail, do you honestly believe that I'll be able to pass myself off as this Joven? Darius may have never met him but there will be someone there who has. They'll tell Darius I am not Joven, and our little charade will be over."

"Joven has never travelled to the east before. No one there will know him," Abigail replied.

He sighed with irritation. "There will be someone. Your need to save this Michael has made you blind to the danger you're deliberately putting yourself in. You and your friends will die a terrible death at the hands of this Darius. Why don't you see that?"

"It's worth the risk," she said.

"Are you in love with this Michael? Is that why you're so anxious to die for him?"

She laughed. "No, I am not in love with Michael."

"I don't believe you." He sounded petulant.

She gave him a look of exasperation. "What is with you, Val? Why are you so sure that I'm fucking or falling in love with every human that crosses my path? First Wesley and now Michael?"

He didn't reply and she stared moodily up at the dark sky. "Neil told me once that vampires were similar to humans, but I've been here long enough now to know that isn't true. You've forgotten what it means to care for someone."

He gave her a wounded look. "That's not true. I care for you."

She shook her head. "No, you don't. You want my blood and nothing more."

"You can't possibly believe that."

She stopped and stared gravely at him. "Why wouldn't I believe it? Last night I would not let you bite me and what did you do? You told me to get out and wouldn't speak to me again."

He stared at the ground. Shame was creeping into him and he fought against it. He had nothing to be ashamed of.

"I'm a vampire, Abigail. You may be doing your best to turn me into a human so you can justify your need to fuck

44

me, but I refuse to be your lapdog. I am not some weak-willed human that you can bend to your will."

"That isn't what I'm trying to do."

"Is it not? You're more than willing to fuck me, but God forbid you should let me feed from you. You used to beg me to bite you remember? Now that you're no longer the scared human you once were, you -"

"Fuck you, Val!" She suddenly shouted. "I saved your goddamn life, remember? And if you had just left me alone, hadn't tried to fucking seduce me, I could have resisted you until we got to Karna."

He snorted derisively. "You were going mad. Everyone could see it. I did you a favour by continuing to feed from you, and you were more than happy to oblige me."

"A mistake I won't make again!" She shouted furiously.

Wesley appeared, frowning and panting lightly. "Are you trying to bring every goddamn leech within ten miles down on our heads?"

Abigail, her pale skin flushed, threw him a furious look. "Let them come."

"All right, calm down, Abby." Wesley reached out to touch her, glanced at Val, and dropped his hands. "Come back to the camp. You need to eat and get some sleep. You hardly slept at all last night."

"I'm fine," she muttered. She glared at Val who set the buckets of water down on the ground before returning her glare.

"You will stay at the camp until I return." He disappeared into the trees.

Abby screamed with frustration and then shouted, "Kiss my ass, you stupid leech!"

Wesley gave her a look of astonishment and then giggled. The girlish giggle coming from such a large man never failed to make her laugh, and she started laughing with him.

"Only you would tell a vampire to kiss your ass." Wesley grinned at her as they each picked up a bucket and started back toward the camp.

———

VAL WATCHED WITH DISGUST AS THE OLD MAN, HE THOUGHT his name was Bill, nodded off once more. This time when his chin hit his chest it stayed there, and large snores emanated from his mouth. It was his turn for watch, and it hadn't been two hours before the old man had started to doze off.

Val jumped down from the branch of the large tree, landing with a soft thud on the ground, and moved silently into the camp. It would be dawn in a few hours. He had thought he would go hunting and had, in fact, stalked a mountain cat for an hour or so. In the end, he hadn't killed it. He had gone back to the camp and made himself comfortable in one of the trees overlooking the camp. He had watched as the humans ate a cold dinner and talked quietly.

He had bared his fangs on more than one occasion when Wesley had sat too close or touched her for no reason, but he reminded himself that Abby would never forgive him if he killed the human. She was obviously very fond of him. Jealousy sang in his veins and he knew that he was hiding himself in the tree because he wanted to know if Abby was fucking the human. He had tensed when they had settled to bed for the night, but Wesley had not gone near her.

He could feel the thirst, but he didn't bother to go hunting again. It was Abigail's blood that he wanted. As he walked past the sleeping Bill, he realized he would rather starve than drink another drop of animal blood.

Abigail was sleeping on the ground, curled up under a light blanket. He looked around almost guiltily before lifting the blanket and sliding in behind her. She was a deep sleeper, and he hoped that hadn't changed.

She didn't move, and he carefully molded his body to hers. She was dressed in her pants and shirt. Although she had removed her sword, the dagger was still around her thigh and the silver gleamed softly around her throat and wrists.

He rested his face against the back of her skull and took a deep breath. God, she smelled good. He wanted to bury his face in her neck, but the silver did an effective job at keeping him away. Instead, he brushed her braid aside and kissed the soft skin just below her ear. He froze when she shifted under the blanket and pressed her ass against his cock. Already semi-erect, it stiffened completely. He stifled a groan when she rubbed her ass against him.

She made another soft sigh and he slipped his hand inside her shirt and cupped her breast through the soft, tight under-shirt she was wearing. Her nipple hardened against his palm and he plucked at it. She arched her back in response, and his pulse thudded heavily when she moaned in her sleep.

He could smell her blood and he licked his lips as his fangs lengthened. He stared at the vein just below her ear and made his own soft groan of need. He was desperate for just a taste of her, and his entire body shivered as he fought the urge to sink his fangs into her skin.

He opened his eyes and stared straight into the tiny face of Violet. He jerked, his hand squeezing Abby's breast, and she frowned in her sleep.

"Gentle, Val," she sighed.

He released his grip, more relieved than he was willing to admit that it was his name she sighed. He stroked her breast as the little pixie gave him a look of disappointment.

"I wasn't going to bite her," he whispered defensively.

She arched her eyebrows at him, and he felt another wave of uncharacteristic shame sweep through him.

"I wasn't," he insisted. "I just – I miss her."

Violet's face softened and she flew forward and brushed her tiny hand across his cheek. His fangs were retreating and the urge to taste Abigail's blood had subsided to a dull roar. Violet petted his face again.

"Tell anyone I said that, and I'll squash you under my thumb," he threatened without malice.

She rolled her eyes and pointed to her throat before smacking him lightly on the chin.

"I'm well aware you're mute," he muttered, "but I've no doubt you'd find a way to tell her if you were determined enough."

She shook her head and kissed Abigail's cheek. Val looked around the camp. Faren was still not back and he rested his head behind hers on the jacket she was using as a pillow. He cupped her breast and pulled her against his body, as Violet landed on his neck and lay across it. He could feel the pixie's wings vibrating against his skin. He stared up at the dark sky as Abigail breathed deeply and rhythmically against him.

CHAPTER 5

Val stared at the ceiling of the carriage and waited impatiently. It had bumped to a stop less than ten minutes ago and he could hear the sounds of the humans setting up camp. Although the thick shutters on the carriage prevented any light from entering, he could sense the fading light of the sun. It would be at least another five minutes before he could leave the carriage. He glanced to his left. Faren was a sleeping lump on the seat across from his.

He closed his eyes and listened carefully. Faintly, he could hear the soft murmuring of Abigail's voice and he relaxed against the seat. By this time tomorrow they would be at Darius' estate. Apprehension slipped down his spine. He had a very bad feeling that Abigail would die at the hands of this Darius, and he was constantly fighting his urge to simply heave her over his shoulder and carry her away from this madness.

Faren stirred and sat up, rubbing his hand through his blond hair. He yawned and sat back against the seat, scratching absentmindedly at his crotch as Val sat up and pulled his boots on.

"What do you think the chances are those idiot humans will have stopped close to a town. God, even a small village would do. I'm tired of deer," Faren said grumpily.

Val rolled his eyes. "You've drank deer two nights in a row. It's not going to kill you."

"Did you feed last night?" Faren asked.

Val shook his head and Faren frowned at him. "Why are you doing this? Seduce the woman and feed from her."

"I told her I wouldn't."

"So? Are you a vampire or not? Since when do we need a human's permission to feed from them?"

"Not all of us feel the need to treat the humans like pets."

Faren shrugged. "If you seduce her first, it won't matter. She'll beg you to feed from her. Hell, you can't tell me she didn't beg you to feed when you fucked her."

"She didn't."

He stared at Val for a moment. "Huh. That's pretty impressive for a human. If you won't seduce and feed from her, perhaps I should. I'm curious to see if she can resist me the way she so easily resists you. I am known for -"

His voice cut out and he made a quiet choking noise. Val had moved across the carriage and was squeezing his throat with an iron-clad grip.

"I told you before. If you go anywhere near her, or near her friends, I will tear your head from your body. Do you believe that I am lying?"

Faren, his face red and his hands clamped uselessly around Val's hand, make a gurgling whisper.

"Do you?" Val repeated and Faren shook his head.

"Good." Val released him and stood in the middle of the carriage as Faren coughed and wheezed.

"Fuck, Val! I thought we were friends," he choked out.

"We are. As long as you remember the woman belongs to me."

When Faren only stared at him, Val leaned forward, his eyes glowing. "I was not lying when I told the dark human I killed the last man who touched her. We're friends, Faren, but I won't hesitate to kill you if you go anywhere near her. Do you -

There was a loud thump as something hit the top of the carriage and the entire thing rocked wildly. Faren was thrown from the seat and Val fell backwards, smashing the back of his head against the rough, thick wood of the shutters.

"What the hell was that?" Faren rose gracefully to his feet.

"I don't -"

There was a loud shrieking cry of pain. Val's entire body tensed before he leaped for the door of the carriage. Faren threw his arms around him and dragged him back.

"Have you gone mad? The light has not yet faded! You'll burn to a crisp, you fool!"

Val cursed loudly as there was another thin, wavering scream from outside the carriage. It was followed by a loud, inhuman roar and every hair on Val's body stood on end.

"Abigail!" He shouted before tearing free from Faren's grip. He ran to the door and held the handle. Wesley bellowed noisily, an inarticulate sound of pain, and Val snarled and pounded on the door in rage.

"Wesley, move!" He heard Abigail shout as the last of the light faded from the sky.

He tore the door open and leaped from the carriage. He stumbled to a stop, staring in disbelief at the scene in front of him.

"Shifters!" Faren hissed beside him.

Val sucked in his breath. Shifters were half-human, half-beast. They were laughably stupid but incredibly dangerous. There were many types. Feline, wolf, and hyena were the most common but bigger, more threatening ones lurked deep within the woods. The shifters who had attacked the camp were bear shifters and some of the largest he'd ever encountered.

As he watched, the largest shifter lumbered its way to where the old man, Bill, was crawling across the grass. The man's leg had been torn into and was hanging by only a few shreds of flesh. Blood flowed steadily from the wound, and Bill made a high-pitched keening noise as the shifter fell on him.

It roared with hunger before swiping its massive paw at Bill. The old man screamed again as the claws sunk deep into the back of his neck. He was turned as easily as a rag doll, and the shifter snarled and buried it's large, hairy head into the old man's neck.

"Bill!" Abigail screamed piercingly as the bear bit through the man's neck, decapitating him. The shifter growled in obvious delight and tore a huge chunk of flesh from the man's upper body.

Val shook off the paralysis that had come over him as Abigail ran toward the now-dead Bill and the shifter feeding from his body. Her sword was drawn, and she leaped nimbly over a fallen log as Val raced toward them.

"Abigail, no!" He shouted.

Behind him, he could hear Faren hissing and growling as he leaped on a shifter that was attacking Evan. There was a loud growl of rage from one of the shifters, and Wesley screamed in triumph as he thrust his sword deep into the shifter's fur-covered belly.

Before Val could reach Abigail, a shifter attacked him from behind. He felt its claws sink into his back and with a snarl of rage he threw himself backward. The claws sunk deeper into his back, but he ignored the pain and slammed his body against the shifter, knocking it to the ground.

He turned nimbly, the shifter's claws tearing from his body, and pinned the animal to the ground. It snapped its teeth at him, and Val hissed as he raised his hand. His fingernails had lengthened and sharpened, and he dragged them across the beast's throat. They sunk easily into its thick pelt and sliced open the flesh and the large pulsing vein beneath it. Blood sprayed from the neck, and the shifter made a soft whimper before shifting to its human form.

Val pushed away from the dying beast, looking frantically for Abigail. His mouth dropped open in disbelief. Abigail, her cheeks flushed, and her eyes lit with a wild fierce light, was battling the largest shifter. He watched as she moved around the hulking beast with the easy, limber grace of a dancer. Her sword flashed in the dim light of the moon as she thrust and jabbed. Each swing of her sword took a piece of the shifter. It roared and screamed with rage as chunks of bloody fur and flesh dropped to the ground.

He realized with a dim kind of amazement that she was actually toying with the beast. It swung one meaty paw at her head, and she dodged it easily before jabbing her sword into its thigh. It roared again and dropped to all fours.

Before it could stand up, Abigail raised her sword and thrust it deep into the top of its head. It dropped like a stone to the ground and Abigail gave a thin shriek of victory before bracing her foot on the shifter's shoulder and yanking the sword from its skull. Panting, her body and face splattered with the beast's blood, she jerked and raised her sword as Val grabbed her arm.

"Abigail, it's me," he said as she stared at him.

After a moment, she lowered her sword. She glanced over at Bill, and a soft moan escaped her lips.

"Oh, Bill," she whispered. Tears were starting to slip down her face and her entire body slumped as she dropped her sword to the ground.

"I'm sorry, little dove." Val put his hand on her shoulder, and she turned and wrapped her arms around his waist, burying her face in his chest.

He hugged her and rubbed her back. Violet, her small face pinched with fear, buzzed up to them and landed on his shoulder.

She rubbed his cheek and he murmured, "She's okay, bug."

Violet squirmed between them and kissed Abigail's neck repeatedly. Abby lifted her head from Val's chest and gave the pixie a wavering smile. "I'm all right, little one."

She stared up at Val and he wiped at the blood that was on her face with the ball of his thumb. She caught her breath and his eyes dropped to her mouth. He dipped his head and her lips parted in anticipation of his kiss.

Before he could press his mouth against hers, Wesley called her name. She jerked in his arms and pulled away from him, and Val hissed at the dark-skinned man.

"Stop it," she admonished as Violet clung to her neck. She looked at her hands, they were covered in fresh blood, and she gave him a wide-eyed look of fear.

"You're bleeding!"

She yanked on his arm and made him turn around so she could examine his back. She made a low moan of dismay at the blood that was seeping through his shirt and tugged at the hem of it.

"Raise your arms, Val," she demanded.

He lifted his arms obediently and she pulled his shirt over

his head as Faren joined them. He peered with interest at the deep punctures in Val's back.

"Not bad." He grinned.

Abigail glared at him. "Make yourself useful and get me some bandages."

Faren rolled his eyes. "I'm not your servant, human."

He walked away, humming softly under his breath, before crouching and prodding at the closest dead shifter. "I have not seen bear shifters in many years. I thought their kind died out long ago."

Abigail traced the wounds on Val's back and frowned when he shuddered. "I'm sorry, did that hurt?"

He shook his head and took a few deep breaths. The wounds were already healing, he could feel the flesh starting to knit back together, and he was uncomfortably aware of the softness of Abigail's hands on his back. It was all he could do to stop himself from turning and kissing her.

"Oh my God," Abby whispered. She watched as Val's skin closed over the puncture wounds. She rubbed away the streaks of blood and shook her head in amazement at the smoothness of his back.

"That's so cool," she muttered, and he grinned before turning around to face her.

"Are you sure you're not hurt, little dove?"

"I'm fine."

Wesley and Evan were crouching over Bill's dead body and she joined them. Val watched as she rubbed first Evan's back and then Wesley's. His hands clenched into fists when Wesley hugged her, his large body shuddering against hers.

"I'm so sorry, Wesley," she whispered.

He nodded and she kissed his cheek. "Let me see your side."

Blood was seeping through his shirt and he lifted it

gingerly. Abby bent and frowned at the slashes on his side. "Oh, Wesley."

"It's not as bad as it looks." He gritted out when she probed gently at the torn skin.

"They'll need to be sewn up." She gave him a rueful look as he dropped his shirt.

She turned to the young redhead. "Evan? Are you hurt?"

The redhead, his freckles standing out from his pale skin, shook his head. "No. The leech saved me."

Faren grinned and gave him a small salute. "You're welcome, human."

The three of them stood and Abigail slipped her arms around Wesley's and Evan's waists and squeezed briefly, being careful not to touch Wesley's wounds. "We need to bury him."

"We should go," Val said. "There may be more."

"We bury him!" Wesley snapped at him and Abigail rubbed his back.

"We will, Wesley."

Val opened his mouth to argue and she gave him a hard look and shook her head. He sighed and walked away.

"VAL, YOU SHOULD GO AND FEED," ABBY SAID.

She was kneeling on the ground next to a stretched-out Wesley. Evan was hovering over them, holding a lantern as close to the big man's side as he could, while Abigail carefully sewed the man's torn skin.

Wesley flinched and muttered a curse and Abigail gave him a look of apology. "I'm sorry, Wesley. I never was very good at this, even with Michael's instructions."

He shook his head. "It's fine. Keep going."

56

She nodded and glanced briefly at Val. "Did you hear me? You should feed."

Faren had left nearly three hours ago. They had buried Bill and then travelled for an hour or so. Val wanted to keep going but Abby had insisted they stop. Wesley's wounds were still bleeding and needed to be attended to.

"I'm not leaving you alone," he replied.

"I can take care of myself." She squinted in the dim light as she slid the needle through Wesley's flesh.

"I've noticed," he said dryly.

"Sometimes I think there would be advantages to being a leech," Evan said.

"Evan!" Wesley frowned at him.

"What?" Evan shrugged. "Look how quickly the leech healed."

"I would rather bleed to death than become a leech," Wesley said.

"Hush," Abby said. "No one is bleeding to death – I'm almost done."

Without looking at Val, she said, "How did you do that, by the way?"

"Do what?"

"Heal so quickly."

He frowned. "Vampires have natural healing abilities."

She paused, the needle and thread held in her blood-covered fingers. "You didn't drink blood though."

He gave her a questioning look and she snorted impatiently. "When you were injured with the silver, your wounds didn't heal. Without blood you would have died."

"Vampires can heal themselves from most wounds within minutes – even without blood. Blood does help us heal faster but it isn't necessary. A well-fed vampire will heal faster than a starving one. Injuries from silver will heal eventually. But if they're bad enough and we aren't given blood to help speed the healing process, we die before we can heal ourselves."

He paused, "Did your Michael not tell you this? I thought he was knowledgeable about my kind."

"He teaches us how to kill your kind," Wesley said. "That's all we need to know."

Val didn't reply and Abby quickly rinsed the smears of blood from Wesley's side. She took the lantern from Evan and held it closer, squinting at her handiwork. "Well, it's done. You're not going to win any beauty contests but you're not going to bleed to death either."

"Thank you, Abby." Wesley squeezed her hand and she gave him a quick peck on the forehead.

"You're welcome."

She washed her hands in a bucket of water as Faren strolled into the camp.

"Val!" He sat down beside the vampire and clapped him on the back. "How are you, my blood-sucking friend?"

Val stared at him suspiciously. "You're suddenly in a good mood."

"Indeed I am." Faren grinned at him. "There is a cabin not twenty miles from here. I suggest you go to it."

"Do you now?" Val said.

"Well, perhaps not the cabin itself, but definitely the barn. You'll find three very lovely and very willing ladies waiting for you."

Abigail sucked in her breath, her hands pausing in the bucket of water, before she pulled them out of the water and dried them briskly on a towel. She rummaged through a small bag and pulled out some bandages to cover Wesley's wounds.

"They're sisters and they're very eager to meet you," Faren said. "The two oldest are a bit...tired but the youngest is ready to go. I told her how handsome you were, and she was quite intrigued."

Abby finished bandaging Wesley's wounds. Without looking at Val, stood and walked to the carriage. She disappeared inside of it as Faren stretched out on the ground beside the fire. Val stood and walked to the carriage.

"Stay away from her, leech!" Wesley stood, wincing a little, and glared at him.

Val ignored him and stepped into the carriage, closing the door behind him. Wesley cursed and started to follow him. Evan grabbed his arm.

"Don't, Wesley. She can take care of herself and besides, she's already slept with him once. She can deny it, but you and I both know she's letting him feed from her. The leech hasn't gone hunting at all and there's no way he would go this long without blood. You don't have a chance with her now, and you know that."

Wesley glanced at Faren, who smiled broadly at him. "Val does like to eat on a regular basis."

"She isn't letting him feed from her." Wesley tried to sound confident but there was doubt in his voice.

Evan shook his head and pulled out some dried meat from a leather bag. "You know that isn't true."

"WHAT ARE YOU DOING, LITTLE DOVE?" VAL ASKED.

Abby was kneeling on the floor of the carriage. There were built-in cabinets under each seat of the carriage, and she was sorting through one of them.

She pulled out a short blue skirt and frowned at the thin, blue piece of material lying underneath it. It was a bikini top, the material so thin it was nearly translucent, and she stared at it in the dim light of the lantern. "What the hell is this?"

"If I had to guess, I would say it's what Joven gives his pets to wear," Val replied.

Her eyes widened and she shook her head. "Ridiculous."

She tossed the top on to the skirt and dipped her hand into the drawer again. This time she pulled out a leather collar, the leather stained blue to match the skirt and top, and she stared at it disbelievingly. "A collar? Are you kidding me?"

Val stared at the collar. The sickness that had wiped out so many of them had also destroyed many of their more common practices, such as keeping humans as pets. However, in the last fifty years the balance had shifted again, and more and more vampires were seducing humans into being their personal meal tickets.

In five centuries of being a vampire, he had never taken a human as a pet. He had seduced them, fed from them, but had always moved on after one night. He found the human's neediness for him after feeding to be more of an annoyance than anything else. Until, that was, he fed from Abigail. From the moment he tasted her blood, he'd been determined to make her his.

He stared at the collar and pictured buckling it around Abigail's neck and claiming her as his own. He was ashamed to realize he had a raging erection. He shook off the feelings of shame. Abby belonged to him and if he wanted her to wear a collar, she would do so.

You don't really believe that. Face it, Val, you may be a vampire but you're not like Faren and the others. You never will be. Not after what they did to Karena.

He moved until he was standing next to Abigail. "Many vampires use collars to show other vampires that the human belongs to them."

He bent and searched through the open cabinet and pulled out a leather wrist cuff. It was stained in the same shade of blue as the collar Abigail was holding.

"There, you see? Joven wears this and his pet wears the collar. It will discourage other vampires from feeding off his pet."

She slid away from him and sat on the seat, rubbing the leather collar nervously between her fingers. "You're kidding me."

"I am not, little dove." He sat down beside her, crowding up against her and blocking her with his arm when she tried to squirm away.

"I'm not wearing this." She glared at him.

"You have no choice." He stroked her thigh with one large hand. "It was you who decided to become Joven's pet, remember?"

"I remember. But you're not Joven, and I won't wear the collar."

He continued to stroke her thigh, his fingers slipping between them to rub the inside of her leg. He could feel the silver band through her pants, and he traced it with his fingers.

"Why are you here anyway?" She suddenly said. "There are three beautiful women waiting for you, remember?"

He grinned at the jealousy in her voice. "Are you jealous, little dove?"

"No."

He moved his head until his mouth was hovering over hers. "You are."

At the feel of his warm breath on her lips, she moaned and kissed him hard on the mouth. She pushed her tongue eagerly into his mouth and he stroked at it with his as she climbed onto his lap. She pulled frantically at the buttons on his shirt, opening them quickly and then bending her head to kiss his naked chest.

He groaned and cupped the back of her head as she kissed his collarbone and then his neck. He cupped her breasts through her shirt, tugging on her nipples as she ground her pelvis against him.

He tipped his head and stared up at the ceiling of the carriage as Abby licked and nipped at his throat. He could smell her arousal, and her blood sang its intoxicating song to him. His fangs lengthened and he made a low, growling noise when she sucked on his earlobe.

"I want to fuck you, Val," she muttered into his ear. "Right now."

He wound his hand into her braid and tugged her head back. "Will you allow me to feed from you, little dove?"

She stiffened on his lap, her hands digging painfully into his chest. "You know I won't."

"Then I won't fuck you," he said.

She gave him a look of disbelief. "Val, I -"

"No. There will be no bargaining with this. I won't fuck you again until you allow me to feed from you."

She shoved her way off his lap and glared at him. "I'll never allow you to feed from me again."

"And I will never fuck you again," he replied.

"Fine," she retorted.

"Fine," he snapped.

She crossed her arms over her chest and scowled at him. "Then I guess we both know exactly where we stand with each other."

"Indeed." He stood up and walked to the door of the carriage. "If you'll excuse me, I have a dinner engagement in the form of a beautiful and willing woman."

He ignored her look of hurt and left the carriage. She

stormed to the door and shouted, "Enjoy your dinner, you arrogant asshole!"

"Which way to the cabin?" Val growled at Faren.

"North, my hungry friend. You won't be able to miss it." Faren grinned as Val disappeared into the forest.

CHAPTER 6

"What's the story between you and the bug?"

Abigail, standing guard at the edge of the camp, ignored Faren's soft voice drifting across the camp. Violet turned on her shoulder and glared at Faren before sticking her tongue out. She twisted back to face Abigail and continued to rub her cheek, giving her a look of pity.

"I'm fine, little one," Abby said. "What do I care if the leech feeds or fucks other women? He's probably fucked a hundred women since I was taken."

Violet shook her head and held her hand up. She made the shape of a zero and stared at Abigail.

"He hasn't slept with another human woman?" Abby said.

Violet shook her head again and then pointed at Abby before making a crying gesture with her fists.

"I highly doubt he was crying over me, Violet. And I'm sure he fed from other women when you weren't around." She sighed and stared into the darkness, listening intently for any strange noises.

She stiffened and drew her dagger, turning to glare at

Faren who was suddenly standing directly behind her. "Don't sneak up on me, leech."

He held his hands up. "Sorry. Won't happen again."

She looked behind him. Wesley and Evan were sleeping lumps around the fire and she glanced briefly at Faren before staring into the darkness again.

He stood beside her and stared at Violet. She stuck her tongue out at him again and he chuckled.

"Will you tell me the story between you and the pixie? Please?" He asked politely.

"I saved her life and she saved mine," Abigail said.

"Why is she not with her own kind?"

"Her voice was stolen from her and they drove her away."

"How was her voice stolen?"

"I don't know. She couldn't tell me," Abby said.

Faren laughed. "You're funny for a human. I can see why Val is so smitten with you."

"He's not smitten with me."

"You don't think so?" Faren raised an eyebrow at her. "He seems rather smitten to me."

Abigail shook her head. "Have you forgotten that he is, at this very moment, fucking and feeding from your barn whores?"

"That seems like a harsh comment to make about your own kind." Faren raised his gaze to the large tree about ten feet in front of them. Although it was very dark, he could clearly see Val sitting on one of the larger branches. He ignored Val's warning look and grinned mischievously at Abby.

"Besides, we don't know for sure that Val is with your – what did you call them – barn whores?"

Abigail snorted. "He is."

"Perhaps. Or perhaps he's simply sitting in a tree like a

giant, pale squirrel." Faren laughed and Abby followed his gaze to a large tree.

She squinted up at the tree, but it was too dark to really see anything. She gave Faren a stony look. "You're an idiot, Faren."

He laughed cheerfully. "There are many who think that."

"Go away. I wish to be alone."

He bowed briefly. "As you wish, human."

———

"WE'RE ONLY A FEW MILES FROM DARIUS' ESTATE. ARE YOU ready?" Wesley asked when Faren and Val descended from the carriage the following evening.

Val nodded as Faren winked at Wesley. "As ready as we'll ever be."

Val turned to Abigail, but she had already disappeared into the carriage. He sighed harshly. She had been ignoring him since the moment he returned to the campsite. He cursed himself in his head for letting his anger get the best of him, but her refusal to allow him to feed from her was puzzling and hurtful. She wanted him to bite her, he knew she did, and her constant denial was driving him mad.

He took a deep breath as Violet flew towards him and hovered in front of his face. She gave him an anxious look and he smiled grimly at her. "It'll be fine, bug."

He looked around the forest. "You should stay here. Hide yourself in the trees until we return."

She scowled at him and shook her head no.

He sighed. "It's going to be dangerous, bug. It's safer for you to stay in the forest."

She shook her head again and landed on his shoulder,

wrapping her limbs around his long hair as though she was afraid he would simply disappear.

He reached up and patted her small back. It was ridiculous how fond he was of the little pest. He ignored Faren's grin as the carriage door opened and Abby descended the short steps. Behind him, he heard the sharp inhale of Wesley and he hissed in response. Not that he could blame the human. His cock had hardened in his pants at the sight of her, and he thanked God that everyone's attention was on Abby.

"Very nice, human," Faren said silkily.

"I look ridiculous," Abby said.

"Ridiculous is not the word I would use." Wesley cleared his throat and ignored Val when he hissed again.

Abby had changed into the slave outfit and Val couldn't stop staring at her. Her long dark hair was unbraided and hung down her back in a dark waterfall. The short skirt and translucent bra left a shocking amount of her creamy skin visible, and she crossed her arms nervously over her torso as her gaze fell on Val.

He strode jerkily to her, stopping when he was only a few inches away, and looked her up and down. His eyes darkened when her nipples, clearly visible through the thin top, hardened noticeably and she immediately crossed her arms over her breasts.

"Stop looking at me like that."

"Like what?" He asked innocently.

"Like you want to eat me for dinner." She gave him another scathing look and he grinned at her, his fangs long and white in the dim light.

"Where is your collar?" He was already wearing the leather wrist cuff.

"I told you – I'm not wearing it," she replied.

He frowned at her. "Abby, the collar has a very specific

purpose. You need to wear it. If you don't, the other vampires will believe you are free for the taking. You cannot - "

"Drop it, Val. I'm not wearing it and you can't make me."

"Abby," Wesley said, "I think the leech is right. You don't want - "

"Be quiet, Wesley." She glared at him. "It's bad enough I have to wear this stupid outfit. I'm not wearing the collar and that's final."

Wesley nodded as Val reached behind her and opened the carriage door. "After you, little dove."

Without speaking, Abby turned and climbed awkwardly into the carriage. The skirt she was wearing was extremely short and Val caught a flash of her white panties as she climbed the steps.

"Little dove?"

"What?"

He indicated for Faren to wait outside and followed her into the carriage before shutting the door behind him. He stared down at her as she glared at him.

"What do you want?"

"Take off your panties."

She gaped at him. "What? No!"

He leaned against the door of the carriage. "No vampire allows their human slave to wear underclothes. It defeats the purpose of the slave."

She snorted with anger. "Pigs."

He shrugged. "Perhaps. I will not force you to wear the collar, although you are safer with it, but I must insist that you remove your panties. Wearing them is a clear sign that you are not under my control. Do you understand?"

She stared at the floor of the carriage, her leg jiggling nervously. He took a step closer. "Do you need my help in removing them, little dove? I'd be happy to lend a hand."

She skittered back and shot him a frosty look. "No. Don't touch me, Val."

He frowned and stepped back as she reached under her skirt and yanked her panties down her thighs. She stepped out of them, rolled them into a ball and stuffed them into a leather bag sitting on the seat.

"There," she said a bit sulkily. "Is that better?"

"Much. Be careful when you sit down – that skirt is delightfully short."

"Thanks for the tip," she replied peevishly.

"I'm only trying to help. I do not want others to see what belongs to me."

"One - it doesn't belong to you and two – do you really think I want a bunch of leeches seeing my goddamn hooch?"

Holding the skirt, she sat down on the seat and quickly opened the thick wooden shutters before staring out the window.

Val opened the door and Faren climbed into the carriage. He sat down opposite of Abigail and grinned at her. "May I just say that you're looking lovely, Abigail?"

"Shut up." She refused to look at him.

She squirmed over as far as she could when Val sat next to her. The carriage started with a jolting thud and she clasped her hands together nervously as Violet flew out from Val's hair and landed on her knee.

She smiled softly at the tiny pixie. "When we reach Joven's estate, I want you to stay in the forest outside of his home, little one. It's safer for you."

Violet shook her head and flew up to hover in front of Abby's face. She pressed her mouth against Abby's lower lip and shook her head again before giving her a pleading look.

"Violet, it is not safe and I don't want -"

Violet clapped her hands together sharply and then reached out and yanked on a piece of Abigail's hair.

"Ouch!" Abby flinched and frowned at the pixie. "Why you little - "

Violet flew to Val and tangled herself in his long hair again, peering out defiantly from the strands of hair at Abigail.

"Val, tell her it isn't safe for her," Abby said.

"It isn't safe for any of us," he replied. "If the little bug wants to go, I will not stop her."

"Asshole," Abigail said before turning to stare out the window again.

"HERE WE GO," FAREN SAID.

They had arrived at Darius' estate. It was surrounded by an enormous stone wall and Wesley had driven the carriage to the massive wooden gate. As they d approached, Val shut the shutters without speaking. Abigail strained to hear the conversation between Wesley and the vampires standing guard at the entrance.

She could hear nothing but soft murmuring and she swallowed thickly. Her stomach was a ball of nerves and she prayed that Wesley and Evan would stay calm. The minutes ticked by and she gave Val a sick look.

"Why is it taking so long? Shouldn't they be letting us in? They are expecting - "

There was a loud clanging noise and she jumped on the seat. Val frowned and slid across the seat until he was pressed against her. He wrapped his hand in her hair and tugged until she was staring up at him. Her lips were trembling, and she resembled the old, timid Abby so strongly that he was tempted to pick her up and carry her away from the madness they were heading into.

"Do not be frightened, little dove," he said as the carriage began to move forward. "I will take care of you."

He stroked his thumb across her bottom lip and her mouth parted invitingly. He was leaning down to kiss her when she suddenly pushed him away. She straightened in the seat and he watched as she closed her eyes and took several deep breaths. When she opened her eyes, the scent of her fear was gone, and calmness radiated from her body.

"I'm not frightened, and I don't need you to take care of me," she said. "I can take care of myself."

"Little dove -"

She shook her head. "I will play the part of your slave, Val, because it means saving Michael but when we are not around Darius or others, I don't want you touching me. Do you understand?"

He scowled at her. "Perfectly, Abigail."

Violet, a distressed look on her face, flew to Abigail and buried herself deep within her hair as Val and Abby continued to glare angrily at each other. Faren leaned forward.

"Well," he said cheerfully, "this should go well. I don't foresee us all dying horrible deaths at the hand of Darius at all."

When neither of them replied, his usual cheerful grin faded, and he gave them both a solemn look. "I get that the two of you have a love/hate thing going on but may I suggest that you," he pointed at Abby, "do a better job of pretending you're obsessed with Val and you," he turned his gaze to Val, "do a better job of pretending that she's nothing more than a tasty snack to you. Otherwise, we're all dead."

"Faren -"

"Shut it, Val," Faren said. "I didn't know Joven, but I've

heard the rumours. He's not known for his kindness to his slaves. If I've heard the rumours, then so has Darius and if you do anything out of character, it's going to make him suspicious. The only way this is going to work is if Darius believes you're Joven, so be Joven for God's sake!"

He said the last in a soft little mutter as voices were heard outside the carriage door. It was pulled open and a dark-haired vampire with light blue eyes and a large, red birthmark covering the entirety of his left cheek, peered in.

"My name is Tavien. Welcome, Joven."

"Thank you." Val pointed to Faren. "This is Faren. He is a close friend."

"Welcome, Faren." Tavien's gaze swept over Abby before he stepped back. "Come. Darius is anxious to meet you."

He glanced up at Wesley and Evan who were standing next to the horses. "Your men may drive your carriage to the stables. They will be fed and shown to the slave quarters, and our slaves will bring your things to your room."

Val stood and taking Abby roughly by the wrist, led her out of the carriage. She blinked in surprise at the large stone castle that loomed in front of them. It towered into the night sky and she strained to see the top of it in the dark. The yard and surrounding areas were lit with torches, and she followed Val in the flickering light to the entrance of the castle.

Without speaking, Tavien led the three of them into the castle. The walls were covered in bright tapestries and as they moved down the corridor, Abby peeked into the rooms they passed. They were filled with large and heavy-looking pieces of wooden furniture, their surfaces gleaming dully in the torchlight. She could feel claustrophobia setting in despite the wideness of the corridor.

She took a deep breath and Val gave her a quick look as they stopped in front of a large door. He squeezed her wrist, whether it was meant to be reassuring or a warning she wasn't sure, as Tavien opened the thick wooden door.

They followed him into the dimly lit room and Abigail glanced around curiously. Like the others, this room was filled with furniture but it was mostly heavy, plush couches and chaises. Vampires were reclining on most of them and nearly every one of them had a slave or two sitting on the floor beside them. She glanced upward. The large room was in the very center of the castle, and she could see some of the human slaves wandering through the open hallways of the upper level.

A female vampire, her upper half completely bare except for thick gold chains layered carefully around her neck, smiled at Val and Faren as they walked by. Her slave, a short, blond man, was staring worshipfully at her. She tugged absentmindedly at his collar as they passed. He ducked his head eagerly under her skirt and buried his face between her legs. Abby stared in shock and the female vampire grinned at her before Val tugged her forward.

They were nearly to the middle of the room now and she watched as a tall, lean vampire rose languidly from a large couch and moved toward them. He almost seemed to float, and she took a calming breath as he stopped in front of them.

He had long black hair and light green eyes and he was, she admitted to herself, absolutely gorgeous. His features were delicate, almost feminine and his pale skin was a startling contrast to his black hair.

Val's hand tightened on her wrist before he spoke. "Good evening, Darius. It is a pleasure to finally meet you."

Darius studied him for a moment. "You are Joven?" His voice was low and musical, and a shiver went down Abigail's back. Violet was hidden deep within her hair and she could feel the pixie's wings fluttering lightly against her scalp.

"I am," Val said. "This is a friend, Faren."

Faren bowed slightly. Darius gave him a disinterested glance before returning his gaze to Val.

"You look different than what I pictured," he said thoughtfully. "From the tales I have heard, I expected someone more," he paused, "brutish-looking."

Val didn't reply and Abby quickly dropped her gaze to the floor as Darius turned toward her. "And who is this lovely creature?"

He stepped closer and she willed herself to stay still when he picked up a strand of her dark hair and rubbed it through his pale fingers.

"She's my slave," Val said.

"You brought only one?" Darius asked.

"I thought it best to travel light. I did not believe it would be wise to draw attention to myself."

Darius traced his finger along her neck. "A slave without a collar. How strange."

He circled around her, frowning slightly before bending down and examining the scars on her back. "What a shame that such loveliness is ruined by this ugliness."

He touched the cross on her back. "Did she do this herself?"

"I don't know. I haven't asked," Val replied.

Darius rested his hand on her shoulder and stared at Val. "You do not strike me as the type who would allow your slave to go without a collar."

Val just shrugged, his nostrils flaring when Darius stepped closer to Abigail.

"I have many slaves, but I am always looking for fresh blood. If your master does not care enough about you to mark you with his collar, perhaps you would like to wear mine?" Darius smiled at Abby.

He leaned in and inhaled deeply against Abigail's neck. "You smell delicious, lovely one. I bet you taste delicious. I look forward to finding out for myself."

Abigail stiffened and raised her eyes to Val. He shook his head and she gritted her teeth and forced herself to stay still as Darius ran his hand down her waist to her hip.

"So lovely," he whispered.

Without warning, his hand slid under her skirt between her thighs and cupped her bare sex. Abigail cried out with surprise and anger and twisted out of his grip. She turned and raised her hand to strike his coldly handsome face. Before she could land the blow, Val had caught her arm. He yanked her away and then his hand was on the back of her neck and he was forcing her to her knees. She squirmed and his hand tightened until she gasped in anger.

Darius raised his eyebrows at Val. "You would allow your slave to strike me after I open my home to you, after I offer you the chance to participate in my business venture?"

"Of course not. She will be punished appropriately."

"Will she?" Darius said. He stared at Abigail and she gave him a look of fury before Val forced her head lower until she was staring at the floor.

"Forgive her impertinence, Darius," Val said. "I have only just purchased her and she still has much to learn."

"Indeed," Darius replied.

He stared thoughtfully at Val. "You are not at all how I expected, Joven. In fact, I am starting to wonder if -"

"Joven! My old friend! It is wonderful to see you again."

Val, his hand still holding Abby firmly in place, turned to see a silver-haired vampire heading toward him. He grunted with surprise when the vampire embraced him firmly and breathed into his ear. "Jaxen."

"It is good to see you as well, Jaxen," Val said smoothly as the old vampire smiled delightedly at him.

"How was your trip? It went well, I trust?"

"Yes. A bit on the long side."

"You must be tired from your journey. Darius, shall I show Joven and his friend to their rooms? I imagine they would like to bathe and rest before dinner." Jaxen smiled at Darius who nodded and stepped back as Val lifted Abigail easily to her feet.

"Excellent. Follow me, please." Jaxen started towards a door at the far side of the room.

Faren gave another short bow and winked at a female slave who was staring shyly at him from a chaise to his right before trailing after Jaxen.

"Darius." Val nodded politely and, still holding Abigail firmly around the back of the neck, followed Jaxen and Faren out of the room.

"My lord." Tavien stood next to Darius.

"What is it?"

"He looks familiar to me."

"The Lord Joven?" Darius raised his eyebrow at Tavien.

"Yes."

"You have never been east before. How would you have met him?" Darius questioned.

Tavien rubbed distractedly at the birthmark on his cheek. "I have never met the Lord Joven. I am sure of that."

"And yet he looks familiar to you."

"Yes. Are you sure that he is who he claims to be, my lord?" Tavien asked.

"No, Tavien. I am not," Darius said.

CHAPTER 7

After showing Faren to his room, Jaxen led Val and Abby down one of the many corridors in the castle. They followed him into a large and luxuriously decorated bedroom, and he shut the door firmly.

"Who are you? What -"

Before Val could finish, Abigail had squirmed out of his grip and launched herself at Jaxen. She hugged him fiercely and kissed him on the cheek as he smiled at her. "I see your plan to become Joven's slave worked."

"Oh, Jaxen." Abby kissed his cheek again. "I'm so happy to see you. We didn't know if you received our last message with our plan or not."

"I did and I promptly sent back a reply letting you know just how foolish I thought the plan was," Jaxen said. "Yet you ignored it."

"We didn't receive it," Abigail said.

Jaxen gave her a suspicious look before putting his arm around her waist and squeezing affectionately. "I believe you. Although I am curious as to what happened to the actual Joven."

"I killed him," Val said.

Jaxen raised his eyebrow. "Oh? Why?"

"Because he tried to take what is mine." Val's eyes dropped to Jaxen's hand resting on Abby's hip and Jaxen chuckled.

"I can assure you that you have nothing to worry about. In fact, my tastes run more toward someone such as yourself."

Abigail grinned as Val gave Jaxen an uncertain look before colour rose in his pale cheeks. She kissed Jaxen's cheek again and smiled at him.

"This is Val. He's," she paused, "an old friend."

Jaxen gave Val a considering look before holding his hand out. "It's nice to meet you, Val. You are a long way from home."

"No further than you, I imagine," Val said guardedly.

"Perhaps." The old vampire grunted with surprise when Abigail's hair moved and Violet poked her head out.

"Why do you have a pixie hidden in your hair, Abigail?" Jaxen asked with a touch of amusement.

"Her name is Violet. She was rejected by her own kind after her voice was stolen from her. I rescued her from a spider's web."

Ignoring Jaxen completely, Violet wriggled free of Abigail's hair and flew to Val. She kissed him on the cheek, and he reached into his pocket and pulled out a piece of dried meat. He handed it to her, and she kissed him again before flying off to the windowsill. She sat on the sill and stared out into the darkness as she ate the meat delicately.

Jaxen, the look of amusement still on his face, watched her until Abigail tugged anxiously at his arm.

"Jaxen, do you know where Michael is? Is he -"

Jaxen clapped his hands together briskly. "Before we talk about Michael, we must discuss what needs to change in order for you to convince Darius that you," he looked at Val, "are indeed Joven, and you, "he stared at Abby, "are nothing more than a smitten slave girl."

Abby frowned. "What are you talking about? I didn't -"

"Be quiet and listen to me, Abby. Where is the collar that marks you as Joven's slave?"

"I can't wear that thing," Abby protested.

"You can and you will," Jaxen said. "One, the real Joven would never allow his slave to go without a collar and two, it will provide you with a measure of protection from the other vampires. You will wear it, Abigail."

"Fine," she muttered.

Jaxen turned to Val. "Darius may not know Joven, but he knows the rumours. He was right – Joven is brutal. He's also unforgiving and much smarter than he looks. He has no love for humans, and he is not known for his compassion. He cares about himself and no other. Do you understand?"

Val nodded and Jaxen studied him closely. "If you are to convince Darius that you are Joven you must hide your affection for the humans."

"I have no affection for the humans," Val growled.

"Do you not?" Jaxen raised his eyebrow at him before glancing at Abigail. "Darius has a more liberal policy with his slaves. It is not uncommon for his men to share the slaves. You must be prepared that -"

"No one else is touching her." Val snapped. "I will kill any who tries."

"Yes, you have no affection for the humans," Jaxen said dryly.

"Jaxen," Abigail said impatiently, "does Michael – does he still live?"

"He does. He has fought in over a dozen fights. Darius is quite fond of his fighting style and he uses him often."

Abigail sighed with relief as Jaxen walked toward the door. "It will be difficult to rescue him, Abigail. In all truthfulness, I fear there is very little chance that any of us will make it out of here alive."

He gave them a weary look. "Dinner will be served in an hour. There will be food for those of us who still like to pretend we are human, as well as a variety of slaves to taste."

He gave Val a solemn look. "I would suggest that you sample a few of the slaves. It will look strange if Joven does not."

"Violet, I want you to stay in the room. Do you understand?" Abigail had made a bed for the pixie from a pillowcase and a small basket and Violet yawned and nodded as she burrowed under the pillowcase. Abby stroked the pixie's soft hair before she completely hid herself away and then turned to Val.

"Are you ready?" She stared expectantly at Val who was stretched out on the bed.

He stood. "I am."

She walked to the door, tugging nervously at her too-short skirt as Val rummaged through one of their bags.

"Abigail."

A scowl crossed her face at the collar Val was holding.

"You heard what Jaxen said."

"Yes, I did." She stomped over to him and turned away before lifting her hair. Her entire body was trembling, and he placed a soft kiss on the back of her neck. She jerked in surprise and turned her head to glare at him.

"Stop it. You are not to touch me, remember?"

Without replying, he slid the collar around her neck and

buckled it at the back. The leather was cool against her skin and she tugged at it.

"Is it too tight, little dove?" Val murmured.

She shook her head before taking a deep breath and turning to face him. "Well, what do you think? Do I look the part now?" She asked bitterly as she stared at the floor.

He didn't reply and after a few seconds she glanced at him. Her breath caught in her throat and she could feel her nipples hardening against the thin fabric of her top in response to the look on Val's face. Her hands were shaking, and she clutched them together against her midsection. Val was giving her an almost feral look of lust and need, and she took a nervous step backwards.

"Don't look at me like that," she whispered.

His nostrils flared angrily. "So not only am I not allowed to touch you, I am not allowed to look at you? Is that what you're saying?"

She shook her head. "No, I just -"

She gasped with shock when he moved towards her with lightning speed and crushed her against his body. She could feel his erection pressing against her and she moaned when he threaded his hand in her hair and pulled her head back.

"You have no idea, little dove," he whispered raggedly, "how difficult it is for me not to bend you over that bed, lift your skirt and fuck you senseless."

He inhaled deeply and a tight grin crossed his face. "Your pussy is wet. I can smell your need. Perhaps you enjoy wearing my collar."

"I don't," she whispered. She could have kicked herself at how weak she sounded.

He grinned again and she shuddered against him when his other hand gripped her ass through her skirt. "You have never looked more beautiful to me than you do in this moment.

Never before have I considered keeping a human as a pet but for you, I would make an exception."

"How sweet," she muttered.

He squeezed her ass again. "You were meant to wear my collar, Abigail."

"It's not your collar. It's Joven's, remember?"

"I remember. I will make certain to act exactly as Joven would act."

"What's that supposed to mean?" She frowned at him.

"Do you understand how strange Darius will find it if I do not feed from you?" He asked.

She stiffened against him. "You can tell him you've already fed from me."

He didn't reply and she gave him a hard look. "Tell him that you don't like to feed in front of others."

"He will not believe that."

"*Make* him believe it."

"You would risk saving your precious Michael just to keep me from biting you? You used to beg me to bite you. Have you forgotten -"

"Don't, Val!" Abby snapped. "Don't you dare try and make me feel guilty. We can rescue Michael without you feeding from me."

He glared at her. "If you had been taken as a slave by the real Joven, he would be feeding from you."

"No, he wouldn't," she replied stubbornly.

He snorted in frustration. "Do you have any idea how foolish you sound?"

"I would have figured something out," she insisted. She knew exactly how stupid she sounded but she carried on gamely. "I wouldn't have let Joven feed from me."

"Bullshit."

She pushed away from him and crossed her arms over her

chest. "It doesn't matter. Joven's not here, you are. And I will not allow you to feed from me."

"Allow me?" Val arched his eyebrow at her, and she took a step back at the dark look of anger on his face. "You and I both know I could easily feed from you if I wanted to."

"I would never forgive you," she replied.

HE HADN'T MEANT TO THREATEN HER. HIS HUNGER FOR HER was making him say and do things he immediately regretted.

Abigail was giving him a look of sorrow mixed with pain and Val's anger deflated.

She was speaking the truth. If he fed from her without her permission, any type of love she might feel for him would disappear. He would lose her and her love forever.

So, you love her now? You once swore that Karena would be your only love. Have you forgotten her so quickly?

He closed his eyes and took a deep breath. He didn't love Abigail. He wanted her, he desired her, and he would let no other touch her, but it wasn't love.

It was infatuation, nothing else.

How easily you deceive yourself.

He rubbed at his forehead wearily and stalked toward the door. "Let's go, Abigail."

"Val -"

She was giving him a look of distrust and he shook his head. "I will not take your blood."

CHAPTER 8

Darius lifted his head from the slave girl's neck. "You do not eat, Joven."

"I prefer to eat in privacy," Val replied.

Darius frowned. "That is odd."

"Is it?"

Darius stroked his slave's bare thigh before slapping it. She stood and moved away from the table as Darius leaned back in his chair and stared at Val across the table. "Yes."

Val shrugged before glancing down at Abigail. She was sitting on a cushion on the floor at his feet and he stroked her hair before smiling at Joven. "I enjoy taking my time with a meal. I indulged earlier in our room."

Darius studied him carefully. "Where did you find her? She really is quite lovely and healthy for a slave."

"I bought her at an auction house."

"She must have cost you a great deal."

"I can afford it," Val replied.

"Indeed." Darius gave him a brittle smile. "I am well aware of your wealth, Joven. It rivals my own."

"Which is why you have asked me to join you in your business venture. Tell me more about it, Darius."

Darius waved his hand. "Not this evening. This evening we will cement our new friendship and enjoy all that we desire to eat. Tomorrow we will watch the games. I believe you will find it most entertaining."

He nodded to a slender blonde woman who was reclining on a chaise near the fireplace. The woman stood and walked quickly to Val. Abigail stiffened as the slave girl smiled down at him. She was wearing a short skirt similar to Abby's and nothing else. In fact, Abigail was the only woman in the room not half-naked and as flimsy as her top was, she was suddenly very grateful for its coverage. Her hands tightened into fists as the blonde slave draped herself across Val's lap and tilted her head back. She stroked his arms and smiled encouragingly at him.

"Eat, my friend. I am more than generous with my slaves," Darius urged.

Val dropped his gaze to the woman's naked breasts before stroking his fingers between them. There was a sharp inhale and he looked down to see Abby staring up at him with a look of anger and hurt in her eyes. He raised his eyebrows at her, and she glared at him before bending her head and studying the cushion she was sitting on.

"Come, my lord. Have a drink. There are many who say my blood is as sweet as honey," the blonde woman purred invitingly.

Val could see the small pin holes scattered across the woman's throat and upper chest. Many of them were lined with a thin layer of blood and he licked his lips as the woman leaned closer and rubbed her naked breasts against his chest.

"Go ahead, my lord," she whispered.

Val dipped his head and inhaled deeply against the

THE VAMPIRE'S LOVE

woman's throat. He could smell her blood and her sudden lust. Although he had not eaten for days, he realized that she held no appeal for him.

He licked her throat and the woman arched her back and made a soft moan of encouragement before placing her hand over his cock. She rubbed him through the fabric of his pants before frowning at the lack of response.

"You do not find me appealing, my lord?" She pouted.

"You are more than -"

The blonde woman gave a squeal of surprise when Abby suddenly jumped to her feet and shoved her from Val's lap. She landed on her ass on the floor and gave her a disbelieving look before jumping to her feet.

"You dare to touch me?" She spat.

"You dare to touch him?" Abigail snarled at her.

"I will rip your throat out for speaking to me in such a manner," the blonde slave said.

"Keep your hands off of him or I'll cut them off." Abigail's face was bright red and her chest heaved as she stared bitterly at the woman. "He is mine and you will not claim him for your own."

"Enough!" Val said.

The slave gave him a small smile. "Forgive me, my lord. I only wish to bring you pleasure. I did not mean to upset your whore."

"Whore?" Abigail shouted. She leaped for the woman, snarling angrily when Val stood and yanked her into his embrace. She gave him a furious look and tried to head butt him. Val jerked his head back before slapping her on the ass.

"I said, enough!"

He returned to his seat, dragging Abigail onto his lap and pinning her arms down. She struggled furiously until Jaxen caught her eye. He shook his head and with a muttered curse

89

she stopped struggling and sat quietly on Val's lap. He slid his hand under her hair and gripped her by the back of the neck before giving Darius a contrite smile.

"Forgive the disruption, Lord Darius."

Darius laughed. "My only disappointment is that you stopped them. For only just purchasing your pet, she already seems rather attached to you."

Jaxen sipped from a glass chalice filled with blood. "Joven is well-known for having his pets become too attached to him. It is a burden he bears with remarkable patience. Perhaps, Lord Darius, it is wise if he does not feed from your slaves. It would not do to have them pining after him when he is here for business."

Faren, a small chubby brunette clinging tightly to him, laughed. "It is true, Lord Darius. I have often had to practically beat the slaves off of him with a very large stick."

Darius snorted before studying Abigail sitting stiffly on Val's lap. "I see you wear your master's collar now. Although with your possessive nature of him, it hardly seems necessary, does it?"

Abigail stared at the table. "It pleases Lord Joven to see his collar around my neck and that pleases me."

"I imagine it does." Darius reached out and stroked her long dark hair. "It's a pity you grow so attached to your master. I too know of many ways to please a woman."

Val's hand tightened on her neck until Abby was certain she would have bruises. She could feel his heart beating fiercely against her back and she stroked his large thigh as she curled into his chest. She placed a warm, wet kiss on his throat before curling her fingers into his hair.

"I desire Lord Joven and no other." She took a deep breath and tugged Val's face to hers. She kissed him deeply, pushing her tongue into his mouth and licking at his as his hand cupped her breast and squeezed hard.

Her face flushed, she pulled away and nestled her face into his neck. His hand squeezed her breast again before he dropped it reluctantly.

Darius gave Val an amused smile. "I have heard a great many things about you, Joven, but I'm beginning to realize that there is still much to learn."

Val smiled thinly as Darius leaned back and clapped his hands together briskly. "The sun will rise soon. Let us finish our meal before we go to our daysleep."

ABIGAIL CAREFULLY EASED HER WAY FREE OF VAL'S embrace. He didn't stir and she slid out of the bed and grabbed her cloak. She hesitated and studied Val carefully. He slept more deeply in his daysleep and she stroked his hair back from his face before tracing his cheekbones with her fingers.

There was a soft whirring and Violet landed gently on her shoulder. She kissed Abby's cheek and studied Val for a moment before smiling at Abigail. She puckered her lips and made a kissing noise and Abby gave the pixie a light tap.

"That will be enough out of you, Violet. I have no interest in Val. He is simply a means to rescuing Michael."

Violet rolled her eyes and shook her head before disappearing into Abigail's hair.

"You should stay in the room, little one. What I am about to do is dangerous."

The pixie pinched her ear and Abigail flinched before sighing. "Fine. But stay hidden."

She buttoned her cloak and with one final look at Val, slipped out of the bedroom.

The hallway was quiet and dark. The vampires were in their daysleep and their slaves would have adapted to the vampires' schedule. Her eyes were burning from lack of sleep and she rubbed wearily at them as she slipped down the wide hallway. After they had retired and Val had fallen asleep, she had waited a few hours. She was tired but her need to find Michael, to assure herself that he was all right, was too strong to ignore.

"Of course, I have no idea where the slave quarters are," Abby muttered to Violet. "Do you think they keep them under the castle? In the movies, the dungeons are always under the castle."

She passed silently through the great room where they had dined with Darius and the others. She eased open the large door and peered into the hallway before walking to the door at the end. Already she was a bit turned around. She thought she might be headed deeper into the castle but for all she knew she could be –

She gave a startled yelp when the door opened and the short, plump brunette that Faren fed from last night, pushed her way into the hallway. She was carrying a large tray that was piled high with bread and she screamed when she saw Abigail.

The tray dropped to the stone floor with a deafening clatter, and both she and Abby winced. The slave girl dropped to her knees and gathered the scattered bread.

"I'm so sorry!" Abby crouched and picked up a few of the loaves. "I didn't mean to startle you."

"That's all right." The girl gave her a timid smile. "Are you lost?"

"A little," Abby admitted.

"Why are you awake?" The slave girl asked. "Do you not sleep with your master?"

"I do. I guess I'm just a little too keyed up to sleep," Abigail replied.

"I am surprised that the Lord Joven does not chain you to the bed, seeing that he only just bought you," the girl said. "My first master kept me chained for months before he was certain that I was too attached to him to leave."

Abby frowned. "The Lord Joven knows I can be trusted, despite our short acquaintance."

"I suppose that's true. You do seem to fancy him quite a bit." The girl gave her a shy look. "He is a very handsome man."

"Is Darius your master?" Abigail asked.

"Oh no. I'm one of the lower- class slaves. I have no master." She raised her head to show her bare neck. "Darius' men share me."

Abigail frowned. "How do you control your need for them once they have bitten you?"

"It can be difficult," the girl admitted. "It is," she hesitated, "strange to find yourself longing after a different man nearly every night."

"You were with Faren last night?" Abigail asked.

"Yes." The girl paused and flushed prettily. "I do hope he chooses me again this evening. He was very kind to me when we retired to his room."

"Do you really have no choice in who feeds from you every night?" Abigail asked.

"No."

"That's awful."

The girl shrugged. "I've been in a lot worse situations. At least here there is a warm, dry place for me to sleep and only a few of Darius' men like to use their fists."

Abigail took her arm and squeezed it gently. "You are beaten?"

"Only occasionally."

"Who beats you?" Abigail scowled.

"Tavien is the worst." The girl shuddered visibly. "Luckily he doesn't pick me often to feed from. He favours the slender ones."

"Tavien? Is he the one with the birthmark?"

The girl nodded. "Yes, he's the Lord Darius' closest advisor. He's got a nasty temper."

"What's your name?" Abigail asked as they finished piling the bread on the tray.

"Sienna."

"I'm Abigail. It's nice to meet you, Sienna." She held her hand out and the girl hesitated before shaking it.

"It's nice to meet you as well." She heaved the tray up, her biceps bulging with the effort, and Abby quickly took one end.

"Here, let me help you with this."

"Oh, that's all right. I can manage," Sienna puffed.

"Don't be silly. I don't mind at all."

The two women carried the tray down the hallway. As they rounded the corner, Abigail realized they were back in the main hall. She could see the front door ahead of them and she gave Sienna a curious look.

"Where are you taking all of this bread?"

"To the fighting slaves." Sienna opened the front door and they stepped out into the bright sunlight.

Abigail's heartbeat quickened as she squinted in the light. "They keep them outside?"

"They keep them in a building behind the main castle."

They walked around the side of the castle and Abigail studied the stone building about ten feet behind the castle. To the left of it a curved stone wall rose up nearly forty feet in the air.

"What is that?" Abby pointed with her chin to the wall.

"That's where the games happen," Sienna said. "Lord Darius had it built two months ago. He calls it the arena. There are rows of seats for people to watch the slaves fight."

"Like the Romans and their damn Colosseum," Abigail muttered.

"Like who?" Sienna asked curiously.

"Never mind." Abigail smiled at her as they approached the building. "Is Darius not afraid that the slaves will escape while the vampires are in their daysleep?"

Sienna shook her head. "It is not possible. They are guarded by bear shifters."

"You're kidding me? Shifters working for vampires?" Abigail said in surprise.

"Yes," Sienna replied. She was starting to look a bit nervous and she gave Abigail a worried look. "Perhaps you should stay out here. The shifters are suspicious of new people."

Abby shook her head. "This tray is too heavy for you. I am not afraid of shifters."

Sienna gave her an admiring look. "I am not sure whether you are the most foolish woman I've met or the bravest."

"I am neither." Abby grinned at her. "Although my mother might have made a strong argument for foolish."

Sienna laughed and opened the thick, wooden door of the stone building. Balancing the large tray between them, the women stepped into the cool darkness. There was a low growling from ahead of them and Abby squinted into the dimness. Her eyes had not yet adjusted to the gloom and she could just make out the dark shape coming toward them.

"Who is this?" A man, he was huge with a dark beard that

hung halfway to his chest and small beady eyes, gave her a suspicious look.

"Just another slave," Sienna squeaked out.

"Is she?" The man leaned forward and sniffed Abigail. "Why is she here?"

"The tray is too heavy for her." Abigail smiled cheerfully at him. "I offered to assist her."

"Does the Lord Darius know?" The bear shifter grunted.

"I am only being helpful, my lord." Abby gave him another smile before touching his arm lightly. "Surely you do not believe I am a threat to such a large, impressive man such as yourself?"

The shifter growled dismissively but stood a little straighter before looking Abigail up and down. "Do you belong to one of the leeches?"

"She does," Sienna said quickly. "She is the Lord Joven's personal slave."

"Is she now?" The shifter leaned forward and sniffed her again. "Have you ever been with a shifter before, girl?"

"I haven't," Abby purred softly. "Not yet, anyway."

"Well, if you ever get tired of being the leech's meal, you come and see me. I have forgotten more about fucking a woman than a leech will ever know."

"That's very kind of you." Abigail gave him a slow smile. "What's your name, handsome?"

"Jeremiah." The bear shifter reached out and squeezed her hip before sliding his hand around to her ass.

"I'm Abigail. It's very good to meet you, Jeremiah."

The shifter grinned at her, revealing large yellow teeth, before squeezing her ass with his hard hand. "You're a little slut then, aren't you?"

Abigail shrugged and stepped away from him. "Will you

open the door, Jeremiah? I'm sure the slaves would like their dinner."

The bear shifter squeezed her ass once more before pulling the ring of keys from a hook on the wall to the right of the door. He opened it and Abigail smiled sweetly at him before following Sienna through the doorway.

CHAPTER 9

A bigail glanced around curiously. They were in a small windowless room that had a small bench to their right and nothing else. Ahead of them was doorway that opened up into a long, wide hallway. Barred rooms lined it and she could see a few grimy fists wrapped around the thick steel bars.

"Do not get too close to the bars," Sienna said anxiously. "Just place the bread on the tray and push it through the opening at the bottom. Each slave is allowed one loaf of bread."

"Is this all they are given to eat?" Abigail asked.

"No. We bring them meat and vegetables in the evening. Lord Darius used to give them only bread, but it made them too weak to fight. They put on a better show when they are given meat."

She led Abigail into the hallway, and they set the large tray on the floor. Sienna moved to the first cell on the left and deposited three loaves of bread on the tray that was placed on the floor in front of it before shoving it through the narrow opening at the bottom of the cell. She smiled briefly at its occupants before moving on to the next.

Abby peered into the first cell on the right. Two of the largest women she'd ever seen were sitting on the floor with their backs against the wall. The bigger of the two had short dark hair and her nose was canted to the left. She grinned at Abby, revealing a mouthful of missing and broken teeth, and Abby gave her a small smile in return.

"You're new." She stood with a lazy grace and moved to the front of the cell. "Look Dalia, fresh meat."

"I see her Ursula," the smaller one grunted. She didn't join her sister at the front of the cell. "Hurry up with the bread, slave. My sister and I are starving."

"Sorry," Abigail replied. She quickly piled two of the larger loaves on to the tray in front of their cell and shoved it through the opening, being careful not to lean to close to the bars. Ursula inhaled deeply.

"You smell pretty."

"Thank you."

Abigail moved to the next cell. This one held four men of varying sizes and they all gave her the same look of weary resignation when she pushed the bread into the cell.

As she stooped to gather more bread, she heard Sienna murmur quietly, "Hello, Neil."

Abigail stiffened and then hurried toward the plump woman. She was reaching into the bars and a soft giggle escaped from her lips as Abby joined her. She breathed a sigh of relief. Neil, his face battered and bruised, was holding Sienna's hand. He brought it to his mouth and kissed her knuckles.

"You're looking lovely today, Sienna."

"Thank you." Sienna gave him a shy look as Neil's gaze drifted to Abby.

His mouth dropped open and he released Sienna's hand before taking a step backwards. "Abby?"

"Neil!" Abby, tears starting to slide down her cheeks, reached through the bars. Neil shook his head in disbelief before stepping forward. They embraced through the bars as Sienna stared at them in surprise.

"Oh, Neil. I'm so happy to see you." Abby stroked the large man's face as he gazed in shock at her.

"Abby, I – I thought you were dead."

"No." Abby shook her head. "Where is Maria? Is she all right?"

"Yes. She's two cells down." Neil looked her up and down. "What happened to you, Abby? You look so different."

Abby smiled at him. "I am different. It's a long story."

"Were you captured by Darius?" Neil frowned.

Sienna cleared her throat loudly. "No. She is the pet of the Lord Joven."

"Oh, Abby," Neil said sadly.

"It's fine, Neil. Do not worry," Abigail said.

"How do you know each other?" Sienna had recovered from her shock and she was giving Abby a mistrustful look.

"We met a long time ago but then I was taken by a vampire," Abby replied as Neil squeezed her hands.

Sienna stared miserably at their clasped hands before nodding. "I will leave you alone."

"No!" Neil dropped Abby's hands and reached for Sienna's. "Do not leave, Sienna. I have waited all morning to see you."

A small smile crossed Abby's face. The look of adoration on Neil's face was plain to see and she squeezed Sienna's arm. "Neil and I are only friends, Sienna. Nothing more."

The woman blushed before returning her gaze to Neil. "Seeing you is the best part of my day."

Neil's grin widened and Abby glanced behind him. There was no one else in Neil's cell except for an old man. He was curled into a ball and snoring loudly, and she leaned closer to the bars and touched Neil's shoulder.

"Neil? I am going to see Maria. I cannot explain at the moment, but I promise you that everything will be different soon. All right?"

Neil studied her before nodding. "All right."

She hurried away as Sienna began to hand out the loaves of bread again. She peered into a cell, her heart thudding heavily when she saw Maria's sweet face.

"Maria!"

"Abigail?" Maria was thinner and her long hair had been chopped into a short, unflattering pixie cut, but she gave Abby a warm smile as she rushed to the front of the cell.

"What are you doing here?" She reached through the bars and touched Abigail's face before glancing at the other two women in her cell.

"Do not come too closely," she warned as the other women scowled at them.

Abby kissed Maria's hands and held them tightly. "I don't have time to explain right now but I promise things are going to be better soon. Okay?"

"Did Val find you?" Maria asked suddenly.

Abby hesitated. "Sort of. He found me a couple of weeks ago."

"Where is he now?" Maria frowned.

"I cannot explain right now." Abigail glanced around warily. "Just trust me that it will be better soon."

Maria nodded and Abigail squeezed her hands again. "I must help Sienna hand out the bread. I will try and visit you again tomorrow. All right?"

Maria gave her a small smile and Abby kissed her hands again. "It will be okay, Maria. I promise you."

She dropped the older woman's hands and moved down the hallway, searching each cell as, behind her, Sienna continued to hand out the bread. Her pulse pounding and her mouth dry, Abby approached the final cell on the right. She peered into it, her breath rushing out of her in a huge rush when she saw Michael sitting against the far wall. His eyes were closed and he appeared to be sleeping.

There were three other men in the cell with him and the largest one leered at her. "Hey, pretty little bitch. Why don't you get on your knees? I have a present for you."

He unbuttoned his pants and pulled his flaccid cock out, waving it at her as the two other men snickered loudly. Ignoring him, Abby cleared her throat. "Michael? Wake up."

Michael's eyes popped open and he stared at her for a moment. "Am I dreaming?"

Abby smiled tearfully at him. "You are not dreaming, Michael."

He stood and made his way to the front of the cell before reaching through the bars. She took his hands and squeezed. "Oh, Michael."

The small man smiled at her. "I'm okay, Abigail."

Abby studied him. He was shirtless and his upper torso was covered in cuts and bruises. A dirty bandage was wrapped around his torso and she could see a large patch of dried blood on it.

She jerked when a dirty hand reached through the bars and grabbed her hair. She was yanked forward, and she gasped in pain when her face slammed against the cold steel.

"On your knees, bitch." The man who had spoken to her earlier shook her roughly. Before she could wrench herself free, Michael had grabbed the man's arm and twisted it violently behind his back.

The man screamed pitifully and fell to his knees. Although he was twice the size of Michael, he gave him a fearful, pleading look. "Please, I'm sorry."

"Touch her again and I'll tear your arm from your socket. Do you understand?" Michael said quietly.

The man didn't reply and Michael yanked his arm higher. He screamed again, a thin wavering noise that sounded ridiculous coming from his large body. "I understand! I understand!"

"Good." Michael released his arm and then patted his head like he was a dog. "Back to your corner."

The man staggered to his feet and retreated, rubbing his arm and casting fearful glances at Michael as the other men chuckled loudly.

"Shut the fuck up!" The man snarled before punching the man closest to him.

Michael turned back to Abby. "You should not be here, Abby. It is too dangerous."

"Do you really believe I would leave you to rot in this cell or be killed?" Abby whispered angrily. "We have spent the last few months devising a way to free you."

"We?"

"Wesley and Evan and me."

"What of Bill?"

"He – he's dead. He was killed by a bear shifter as we were traveling here."

Michael's shoulders slumped, and Abby rubbed his arm. "Michael, look at me."

He raised his dark brown eyes to hers and she smiled at him. "It is not your fault. He wanted to rescue you."

"Abby, this Darius is very dangerous." He studied her outfit, his eyes lingering on the collar around her neck, and she blushed a little before crossing her arms over her chest.

"I know. Don't worry. Everything will work out."

She leaned closer as Michael rested his head against the bars of the cell.

"Jaxen will help us and there is another vampire who will help us as well," she breathed into his ear.

"Who?"

"Val."

Michael gave her a surprised look. "The one who saved your life when you first came to our world?"

"Yes."

"Are you allowing him to feed from you again, Abby? You know how dangerous that is. You cannot allow him to bite you even if it means saving me. Do you - "

"He's not feeding from me." Abby whispered. "Do not worry, Michael."

Sienna had approached them, and she gave the two of them a curious look as she slid the tray of bread into the cell. "Do you know everyone here, Abby?"

Abby shook her head and stepped back. "No, Sienna."

Sienna took her hand. "We must leave now. If we linger any longer, the shifter will grow suspicious."

"All right." She reached through the bars and squeezed Michael's hand again. "Stay strong, Michael."

"Be safe, Abigail," he replied.

"I will be." She gave him a reassuring smile as Sienna tugged on her hand and led her back down the hallway.

As they passed Neil's cell he reached out and snagged Sienna by the arm. She smiled sweetly at him as he caressed her pale skin. "I will see you tomorrow?"

"Yes." She hesitated and then leaned forward. Neil's face was pressed against the bars and she placed a quick kiss on his cheek. "Bye, Neil."

"Goodbye, Sienna."

"Sienna? You cannot tell anyone that I know Neil and the others, all right?"

Sienna had led Abby back to Val's room and Abby placed her hand on the woman's arm.

Sienna didn't answer and Abby gave her an anxious look. "If you say something, it will mean Neil's death. Is that what you want?"

Sienna shook her head. "No, of course not! I will not tell anyone."

She hesitated and then gave Abby an anxious look. "Are you sure that you and Neil are only friends?"

"Yes. I promise you. We are nothing more than friends," Abby said. She patted the woman's arm. "Are you in love with him?"

Sienna shrugged. "I don't know. I am very fond of him. He has such a kind manner, does he not?"

"He does. He's a good man, Sienna."

"He seems to be." She sighed softly. "It is difficult for me to know what I truly want. The nights that I am fed on by a leech, I am certain that it is that leech I want and need and that I cannot live without them. But then I see Neil and I…"

She trailed off before sighing again. "I hate that I am attracted to the leeches when they bite me. I feel like I am being unfaithful to Neil. Isn't that ridiculous? I really know nothing about him and I'm not even certain that he is attracted to me. I've had only a few conversations with him but the way that he looks at me – like I am more than just a meal – makes me happy."

"Believe me – Neil is attracted to you." Abby smiled at her. "I have never seen him look at a woman the way he looks at you."

Sienna smiled tentatively. "Truly?"

"Yes, truly." Abby hugged her impulsively. "Please, Sienna. Promise me that you will not say a word to anyone about me knowing the others."

"I won't," Sienna said solemnly. "I promise."

"Thank you." Abby hugged her again before slipping into her room. Despite the bright sunlight, the shutters and thick curtain blocked the light effectively and she waited patiently for her eyes to adjust.

Violet slipped out from her hair and Abby smiled when the pixie glowed brightly and provided enough light for her to see the bed.

"Thank you, little one. And thank you for staying hidden." She followed the pixie's bright glow to the bed and quickly climbed in beside Val as the pixie flew to her bed by the window.

Abby lay in the darkness, listening to Val's rhythmic breathing. Her mind was a whir of happiness and worry. She was thrilled to see Neil and Maria and Michael, but she had no idea how they would rescue them. She sighed and turned on her side, tucking her hand under cheek. She would have to talk to Sienna tomorrow and find out where the slave quarters were. She needed to speak to Wesley and Evan, needed to let them know that Michael was alive, and –

She jerked when Val turned over and wrapped his arm around her. He pulled her into his embrace and threw his large thigh over hers, pinning her to the bed as he buried his face into her hair. He muttered something she couldn't hear before kissing the back of her neck. She inhaled sharply when his hand slid inside her top and he cupped her bare breast.

She squirmed a little but quickly gave up when it only made Val's arm tighten around her. She yawned and relaxed into his embrace. There was no harm in allowing him to sleep so closely to her. He was in his daysleep and would not wake. Besides, it was comforting to feel his warm body against hers, and his presence soothed her and helped to quiet her racing thoughts. She closed her eyes and drifted.

CHAPTER 10

V al opened his eyes and stared at the sleeping woman in his arms. She was tucked against him, her ass pressed firmly into his crotch, and he was cupping her bare breast. He rubbed her nipple, smiling with satisfaction when it hardened, and kissed the side of her neck. She frowned in her sleep and made a soft snorting noise before pulling away from him and burrowing deeper under the covers.

Val flipped onto his back. He stared blankly at the ceiling as he listened to Abby breathe. Even with Jaxen's endorsement, Darius did not believe he was Joven and he had no idea how to convince him he was. He was doing a terrible job at being Joven and he was fairly certain that if he did not drink soon in front of Darius, the vampire would have both him and Abby killed.

Unfortunately, the thought of drinking from another woman, of fucking someone other than Abigail, made him feel ill. He had to figure out a way to convince Abby to let him feed from her. He wanted her and only her, and not even the fact that he was growing steadily weaker by the day was enough to make him drink from another. He realized with soft wonderment that he would rather starve than feed from any human but Abby, and icy tendrils of fear slid down his back. What was happening to him? He could not remember ever feeling this way before, not even with his beloved Karena, and he was –

He stiffened, sitting up in the bed and cocking his head toward the door. His hearing was excellent, and he could hear the distinct footsteps of Darius and another. He knew without a doubt that they were headed to his room and he stared down at Abigail as an idea formed in his head. As the footsteps grew closer, he flipped her onto her back and shook her roughly.

"Little dove! Wake up!"

Abigail muttered and tried to pull the blanket over her head. He pulled it from her grip and she made a soft mew of discomfort when the blanket was yanked down her body and the cool air washed over her.

"Abigail, wake up!"

She stared blearily at Val as he slid down her body. His face was only inches from her core and she stared in confusion at him. "What are you doing?"

"He's coming. Moan for me, little dove," Val said in a fierce mutter.

She tried to pull away from him and he cursed before yanking her thighs apart.

"Stop it! What are you - "

Her indignant cry turned into a moan of pure need when Val pushed her short skirt up, shoved his face between her thighs and licked her pussy.

"Oh my God!" She cried out as her hips arched up off the bed. His tongue slipped between the lips of her pussy and stroked her clit. He sucked hungrily on it and was rewarded with a surge of wetness. She moaned and writhed on the bed, her thighs clamping around his head as her hand gripped his hair and she pushed him more firmly into her.

He pushed one long finger into her hungry pussy and groaned at the way it tightened around his finger. He sucked her clit again and she made another desperate mewling noise of pleasure. He heard the bedroom door opening and he increased the pressure of his lips until she was thrusting her pelvis mindlessly against him.

"Please, oh please!" She cried out. He made a sigh of regret and moved his mouth to her inner thigh. He kissed the soft skin and then bit the inside of his bottom lip, letting his fangs sink deep into his own flesh. Quickly, before the wound could heal itself, he allowed the blood to spill out of his mouth and down his chin.

"I do so hate to interrupt such a beautiful sight, but I was hoping you could join us for an early dinner." Darius' voice broke through Abigail's haze of desire and she shrieked and scrambled back on the bed, closing her legs and shoving her skirt down as Val sat up.

She stared wide-eyed at Darius and Tavien as Darius' eyes glowed at the sight of the blood dripping down Val's chin.

"I see you've already eaten." He licked his lips and looked Abby up and down. "Perhaps you would like to share?"

Val wiped the blood from his face. "No, I would not."

Anger flickered over Darius' face and then quickly disappeared. "A shame. Here in the west we have a much more liberal policy when it comes to our pets."

Val didn't reply. From the corner of his eye he could see Abigail, a look of shock on her face, reaching down to touch her thigh. His hand shot out and grabbed her wrist, squeezing it until she gasped.

"Not to be rude, Darius, but I'd like to finish what I started." His eyes travelled over Abby's pale and shocked face. "I will join you shortly."

Darius looked Abby up and down once more. "Finish tasting your flower's sweet nectar quickly. There will be games tonight."

He and Tavien left the room and Val released Abby's wrist.

She stared wide-eyed at him. "You – you bit me?"

He shook his head. "No. Check for yourself."

Her hand trembling, she reached down and smoothed her hand across her thigh. Blood marred her skin but there was no bite mark and she gave him a look of confusion.

"You bit yourself? Why?"

He gave her an angry look. "I wanted Darius to believe I was feeding from you. In case you didn't notice, he finds it odd that I will not bite you in front of others."

She didn't reply and he stalked away. "Get ready to go."

"We have games three nights a week. We used to hold them every night, but we were running out of slaves too quickly." Darius grinned at Tavien as they led Val, Faren and Abigail outside.

They approached the curved stone wall and Abby could hear shouts of laughter and the loud murmur of a crowd as Tavien opened a thick wooden door. They entered into the arena and Abby stared at the large crowd of vampires that lined the arena. Hundreds of torches were embedded in the wall and the arena was well-lit, despite the darkness pressing in around them. The rows of seating rose high into the air, to the top of the stone wall, and were separated from the arena by a second curved wall. This one was about chest high on her and, as Darius and Tavien led them to their seats, she gave Val a quick glance.

He was staring disinterestedly at the crowd, his face unreadable and she squeezed his hand briefly. He glanced back at her and she gave him a small smile. He didn't return her smile and she bit at her bottom lip before following him into the seating area.

Unlike the rows of plain wooden benches, this area had large fabric armchairs and Darius and Tavien sat down as Darius waved his arm at Val and Faren.

"Sit. Make yourself comfortable."

Val and Faren reclined in the chairs and Abby sat down on the large pillow placed on the floor at Val's feet. Val rested his hand on the back of her neck as a slave girl, this one a redhead, entered their section and smiled eagerly at Darius. "Hello, my lord."

"Sit." He patted his lap and she reclined on his lap before lifting her chin and baring her throat. Although he had just finished eating, he buried his fangs into her soft flesh and drank deeply.

Abby could feel Val's hand tightening around her neck, and she gave him a nervous look. He was watching Darius feed, the hunger apparent on his face, and she felt a moment of guilt. She shook it off. She did not need to feel guilty for not allowing Val to feed from her. It was not his right and besides, Darius was more than willing to share his slaves. He could feed from another if he was truly desperate.

Jealousy surged through her at the thought and she tamped it down. Val did not belong to her and it would be better for her if he did feed from another. It would stop his hunger for her. Still, the thought of Val feeding from another woman, of touching her and fucking her, made her insides burn. She forced herself to stop thinking about it as Darius, his teeth dripping with blood, smiled at Val.

"This one is particularly delicious. I can never resist her."

Val smiled thinly at him before looking away. The woman on Darius' lap purred happily and pressed her curvy body against him. "Thank you, my lord. It is my honour to have you feed from me. I love -"

With an impatient grunt, Darius pushed her from his lap. She fell to the floor with a harsh thud, flinching as her knees missed the pillow and banged against the hard ground.

"Enough. Quiet your tongue or I'll give you to Tavien for the night," Darius said.

The woman paled noticeably and huddled against Darius' leg. "Forgive me."

Darius rolled his eyes and pushed her away from his leg before glancing at Val. "Do you see how popular this has become?"

"Indeed. I have never seen so many vampires gathered in one place."

"They come from miles around to watch the games. And all of them more than willing to pay to watch," Darius said.

"How much do you charge?" Val asked.

"A hundred gold pieces for the front row seating, such as ours. The price lowers as they sit further back but even those vampires sitting there," he pointed to the row of seats at the top of the wall, "pay ten gold pieces for the privilege of enjoying the games."

"Impressive," Val replied.

"We will also accept humans as payment." Darius grinned. "We hold four games at every showing and the humans must fight to the death, so you can imagine how quickly we go through them."

"What happens if they do not fight or refuse to kill one another?" Faren asked.

Darius chuckled as Tavien made a grunt of amusement. "They always fight. They have no choice. If they do not fight each other, we kill them – slowly and painfully. Besides, there are rewards for winning the games."

"What kind of rewards?"

Darius shrugged. "Usually it's more food but occasionally we give them a room for the night, a woman or man to fuck, and a chance to sleep in a real bed."

"Where do you keep them?" Val frowned at him.

"In the stone building we passed. Occasionally, if there is an overflow of slaves, we chain them to the wall of the castle. That, however, has only happened once or twice. Is that not right, Tavien?"

"Yes, my lord." Tavien was studying Val and Val gave him an irritated look.

"Why is it that I find you staring at me so frequently, Tavien?"

"You look familiar to me, Lord Joven. Have we met before?"

"I'm quite certain we haven't," Val replied.

"I think it's time we started the games," Darius said. He rose to his feet and held his arms up. The crowd quieted and Darius smiled.

"Welcome, friends!" He shouted. "I know many of you have travelled a great distance to see the games and I promise you – you will not be disappointed!"

The crowd roared in approval, stomping their feet and clapping their hands as Darius waved his hand at the two vampires in the arena. They crossed to a second wooden door and unlocked it as Darius turned to Val.

"We provide them with a variety of weapons to fight with

and we also do hand-to-hand combat. Those ones last the longest and are always the most popular. There's something about watching a man kill another with his bare hands that pleases even the most cynical of viewers."

Abigail leaned forward, the stone wall in front of them was making it difficult to see from her spot on the floor. Val's hand tightened on her neck before he reached down and lifted her onto his lap.

Tavien was still staring at them and she curled into Val's body before placing a soft kiss on his throat and giving him a worshipful smile. "Thank you, my lord."

He nodded and she kissed him again before the loud roar of the crowd drew her gaze back to the arena.

The large woman named Ursula had entered the arena and she raised her arms into the air and grinned as the vampires cheered.

"This one's always a crowd favourite," Darius said. "A most remarkable woman, wouldn't you agree, Tavien?"

"Yes, my lord."

"We captured her and her sister in an orchard to the south. They gave us quite a battle, did they not, Tavien?"

"They did."

Darius laughed. "It took four vampires to subdue them without killing them. Since then, they've both proven to be quite skilled at the games. Although I believe that this one is the stronger of the two."

He looked up as Jaxen entered their section. "Jaxen! Just in time. Have a seat next to Lord Joven."

Jaxen nodded and sat down next to Val. "Good evening, Lord Joven. Faren, how are you?"

"Jaxen," Val replied as Faren nodded to Jaxen.

"I was just telling the Lord Joven that this big bitch is one of our best fighters. Wouldn't you agree, Jaxen?"

"I would. She seems to have a working knowledge of nearly every weapon we provide her with."

"That she does," Darius answered. "How on earth a simple farm girl like herself knows how to use these weapons, remains a mystery. We tried torturing her for the information but neither she nor her sister would reveal anything. They really are quite remarkable."

He turned back to the arena as a second woman entered the ring. He groaned with disappointment and frowned at Tavien. "I thought I told you to match them more fairly."

The woman who had entered the arena was small and thin. Even from her spot on Val's lap, Abby could see the way her slender body trembled, and she stiffened as the two vampire's handed both women large, wooden clubs.

"We tried, my lord," Tavien answered. "There are not many of the women amongst our current slaves who match her in size or strength. Her sister, perhaps, but I did not think it would be wise to pit them against one another. They would most likely try and turn on the crowd before each other."

Darius sighed irritably. "We need to find larger women to fight. Do not think I haven't noticed that your hunters are bringing back the easiest prey to capture. Women who are small and weak make for a boring game. The next time a party is sent out hunting they would be wise to put more effort into finding suitable candidates for the games."

"Of course, my lord."

Darius sighed again. "The only issue you'll find, Lord Joven, is acquiring enough slaves to fight in the games. Once word spreads among the humans in your area, it will only become increasingly difficult to find suitable ones. As time goes on, we've had to travel further and further to find them. That is why it's excellent business practice to accept humans as payment to watch the games. Have your audience do your work for you."

"It is a rather ingenious idea, Lord Darius," Val replied.

"Isn't it?" Darius preened. "One must always look at all ways to capitalize on their business."

He stood and held his arms up again. A hush fell over the crowd of vampires and they stared at him expectantly. He smiled at the slaves in the middle of the arena. "Begin."

Abby, her heart thudding in her chest, watched as Ursula stalked toward the terrified woman. She was swinging her club in one meaty fist and the woman cried out in terror when she swung it at her. She ducked, barely missing the blow, and staggered back. She took a half-hearted swing with her own club. It glanced off of Ursula's hip and she bellowed laughter before raising her club.

The woman screamed and Abigail cringed as Ursula slammed the wooden club into the woman's right arm. It broke with a loud crack and the woman screamed again hoarsely as her own club fell to the ground.

Ursula, grinning hugely, swung the club again. This time, it connected with the woman's skull and she crumpled to the ground, blood spraying from her skull to splatter on the ground.

Abby made a small moan of dismay and stared down at her lap as Val rubbed her back. He was tense beneath her and she stole a glance at his face. There was nothing on his face to suggest that he was sickened by it but as their gazes connected, she could see the repulsion in his eyes. She looked back down at her lap as the crowd screamed and cheered. Despite the noise, she could still hear the horrible wet thuds as Ursula beat the smaller woman to death.

She clenched her fists and breathed harshly through her nose as Val continued to rub her back. Darius laughed.

"Your slave is too squeamish for the games, Lord Joven."

"It would appear so," Val replied.

"Ahh, the last game of the night. This will be a good one. This particular human is another crowd favourite," Darius said.

Abigail, her stomach churning and her hands ice cold, swallowed thickly. They had been forced to sit through two more games, each bloodier than the previous, and she had spent most of them staring fixedly at her lap.

As the crowd's cheering grew to a monstrous level she took a deep breath and raised her gaze to the arena. A harsh moan escaped her lips and she started to scramble from Val's lap. Quickly, he wrapped his arm around her waist and hauled her back against him.

"Be still," he said in her ear as Tavien stared at them curiously.

Abby glanced at Jaxen. The vampire's face was composed but she could see his hands digging into the wooden arms of the chair he was reclining in. He gave her a small nod, and she forced herself to relax against Val as Darius leaned forward to stare at Jaxen.

"What is this one's name again, Jaxen? Do you remember?"

"I believe it is Michael, my lord."

"Ahh, that's right."

Val stiffened and then leaned forward, keeping Abby firmly on his lap. He studied the small, trim man standing calmly in the middle of the arena. He looked to be in his thirties, and he was shirtless. His upper torso was covered in bruises and old scars and he was barefoot.

Abby was staring at Michael with a terrified look on her face and he squeezed her waist harshly before placing his mouth at her ear. "Hide your emotions, Abigail, or it will be us in that arena."

She nodded without taking her gaze from Michael. Irritation flooding through him, he held her chin and turned her face toward him. "Do you hear me?"

"Yes," she muttered. Already her gaze was sliding back to her beloved Michael and he could barely hold in his snarl of jealousy. He squeezed her chin and, before she could react, kissed her deeply. She twitched in surprise and he continued to kiss her until her body relaxed slightly.

"Remember who you belong to," he breathed against her mouth before sitting back in the chair.

"This one is exceptionally good with a sword," Darius said as he hoisted the slave girl from the floor and back onto his lap. He cupped her breast, toying absentmindedly with her nipple, before dipping his head and drinking from her throat. The girl moaned in delight, her hands gripping his arms as he feasted, and arched her back.

Darius wiped his mouth and pushed her back to the ground, ignoring her soft cry of dismay. He gestured to the vampires in the arena and they handed swords to Michael and his opponent.

Abby studied Michael's opponent. He was tall and blond with the hands of a farmer and a sunburned face, but he held his sword with the ease of one well-practiced, and nodded to Michael.

Michael returned his nod before raising his sword. Abby jerked on Val's lap at the first clash of their swords and he squeezed her thigh tightly and gave her a warning look. She forced herself to relax as Tavien raised his eyebrows.

"It appears your slave has gotten over her squeamishness, Lord Joven."

"I have no doubt at the first sight of blood, it will return," Val said.

Abby ignored them both as Michael and his opponent moved swiftly around the arena. Their swords struck repeatedly, sparks flying from the edges of the blades, as neither one was able to break through the other's defense.

"This is turning out better than I thought." Darius raised his voice over the roar of the crowd. "Normally this one kills his opponent within minutes. Perhaps we have finally found an opponent who is worthy of his -"

There was a gasp from the crowd and Darius fell silent as Michael's sword pierced the stomach of the blond man. The man fell to his knees as blood poured out and darkened the ground around him.

Darius made a grunt of irritation. "It would seem I spoke too soon."

Michael bent and clasped the larger man's shoulder. He whispered in his ear as Darius snorted angrily and stood.

"Finish him!" He bellowed.

The crowd screamed and then echoed Darius' shout. Chants of "finish him", "finish him", filled the arena. Michael ignored them and continued to speak into the dying man's ear. After a few moments he stepped back and raised his sword. The crowd's chanting faded away as they waited for the final blow.

Her throat burning, Abby watched as Michael gave the man in front of him a look of sorrow.

"I am sorry, my friend." His voice was soft but audible in the sudden silence.

Abigail bit the inside of her cheek as he swung his sword

and decapitated the blond man. His head fell to the ground with a soft thump and the crowd screamed raucously, stomping their feet and clapping their hands. The guards returned and took Michael's sword before leading him out of the arena.

Abigail collapsed against Val. Her heart was thudding heavily in her chest and she was close to vomiting. She curled into Val, hiding her face in his throat under the pretense of kissing him, so that Darius and Tavien would not see her emotions.

He stroked her back as Darius stood and hauled his slave girl to her feet. "Come, Lord Joven. You and Faren must join us in the common room. It is our custom to have a gathering for some of our more honoured guests."

CHAPTER 11

Abigail sat stiffly on Val's lap and tried to ignore what was going on around her. They had been in the common room for the last two hours as Darius and about fifty other vampires feasted on their slaves voraciously while they mingled. In the last half hour, the festivities had become more decadent. While she didn't consider herself a prude, she was becoming increasingly uncomfortable with the dark desire the vampires were indulging in.

Even Jaxen was participating. The old vampire had spent most of his time sitting with Val, but he had wandered away about five minutes ago. She watched as he took the hand of a man wearing a dark red collar and led him to a chaise in the far corner of the common room. The slave knelt at his feet and she looked hastily away when he undid Jaxen's pants.

Her gaze landed on Faren and she was relieved to see that he had chosen Sienna again. The brunette was lying on his lap, her hand kneading his crotch and her eyes closed in ecstasy as he fed from her.

She could feel Val's cock hard and hot beneath her. She wasn't surprised. All around them, the vampires in Darius' household were being pleasured by their pets. The thought of public sex had never really appealed to her but as she watched one of the women lift her skirt and straddle the vampire beneath her, she realized wetness was dampening her thighs. The wetness grew when the vampire guided his cock into the woman's pussy, and she gave a loud squeal of pleasure and ground her hips down.

Darius was watching her. His hand was wound through a woman's hair as she knelt between his thighs and sucked enthusiastically on his cock. Her breathing shallow, she unconsciously pressed her ass against Val's cock, and he groaned. Darius was still staring at her and she knew that he was wondering why she and Val were not joining in on the orgy around them.

Val's hand was suddenly on her head and he drew it down to his mouth. His voice rough with need, he whispered, "In a few minutes you're going to tell me that you're not feeling well. Say that you feel sick to your stomach. I'm going to slap you and be angry with you, before I drag you out of here. Do you understand?"

She nodded as her gaze returned to the woman bouncing on the vampire's cock. She knew what Val was doing for her. She knew that he believed deep down she was horrified and would take any excuse to leave.

She took a deep breath. She also knew that no matter how realistic Val made his anger with her look, Darius would not fall for it. If they left now, without Val proving to Darius that she truly was under his control, he would kill them both before the morning. She took another deep breath as Val pushed lightly on her back. She turned to him and smiled before kissing him on the mouth.

He gave a grunt of surprise, but his hands were already circling her waist and he was pulling her against him as she explored his mouth with her tongue. She ran the tip of it over his fangs and then sucked hard on his lower lip before gazing at him.

He was staring at her, his eyes glowing with surprise and lust. She gave him another slow smile before sliding off his lap to the floor at his feet. She knelt between his legs and reached for the buttons on his pants. She flicked them open, keeping her eyes on his face. As turned on as she was, she was afraid she would lose her nerve if she looked around the room. She blocked out the sounds of the moans and groans coming from all around her, and smiled up at Val before licking her lips.

"Little dove," he whispered.

She pulled his cock out of his pants and without speaking, leaned forward and wrapped her lips around the head of it. She suckled hard and ran her tongue over the slit, licking away the drop of precum that dripped out of it.

He groaned and knotted his hands into her hair. He pulled, urging her to take more of his shaft into her mouth. She rose up a little and slid her mouth down his cock until the head of it brushed the back of her throat.

He moaned, staring down at her with eyes burning with lust, and petted her long hair like she was a cat. "Such a good girl, little dove."

She sucked harder in response, darting her head back and forth as she pumped the base of him with her hand. His hips rose and his hand tightened almost painfully into her hair before he made himself relax against the chair.

She sucked on just the head of his cock, and then licked the thick vein that ran underneath the shaft. He groaned and cried out with pleasure before whispering, "Take more. I want you to take all of my cock into your pretty little mouth."

She hesitated and sat back on her heels. She stared up at him and he stroked her face encouragingly. "Try, little dove."

She nodded and slid her mouth over his cock once more. She angled herself over him and slowly moved her head downwards. His cock brushed up against the back of her throat and instead of pulling back, she took a deep breath through her nose and relaxed her throat. She swallowed and swallowed again, pulling more of his cock down her throat until she realized with a soft kind of wonderment that her lips were touching his pubic hair.

She moved up and down, sucking hard, her cheeks hollowing with the effort, his soft groans encouraging her to keep going. She could feel his cock swelling in her mouth and his hands gripped her head as he gave a hoarse shout and came in her mouth. She swallowed his warm seed, her mouth milking his cock until she had pulled every drop from him and he was shuddering beneath her.

She pulled her mouth away, taking deep breaths and biting her lip compulsively as she squeezed her thighs together. Her pussy was dripping wet and pulsing and throbbing heavily, and she had never wanted to come so badly in her life.

He pulled her up off her knees and onto his lap. He kissed her hard on the mouth, his hand slipping into her bikini top to cup her breast. His fingers pulled at her nipple and she moaned. His mouth slipped to her throat and she lifted her head as he sucked and licked at the sensitive skin. His hand crept between her thighs and she spread them eagerly.

She was only vaguely aware of the other people in the room, of their own soft cries of need and pleasure. She made a loud groan of frustration when Val's hand slipped out from between her thighs without touching her pussy.

"Please!" She cried, looking down at him. He was staring

across the room and she followed his gaze. Some of the others had finished and were lying sated on the couches or the floor of the large room. Still others were in the midst of fucking and she watched as a few of the couples left the large room for more private quarters, their hands groping and squeezing each other's flesh.

Darius, his hips pumping furiously as he fucked the woman bent over one of the low couches, was watching them. His gaze travelled over Abby's body, his eyes dark with lust, and a tremor of nausea went through her.

Val lifted her off his lap, standing and doing his pants up before taking her by the arm. He nodded to Darius who gave him a clear look of disappointment. Val marched from the room, dragging Abby with him.

They walked silently toward their room. Away from the gaze of Darius, Abby's lust returned. She wanted to cry with frustration. Once they got to their room, Val would close off from her again and she would be left with nothing but her own need.

They reached their room and Val pushed her into the room before slamming the door shut behind him. She stood by the bed, her entire body trembling with need as he walked to the fireplace and stared silently into the flames.

"Why did you do that?" He asked hoarsely.

"Because," she swallowed hard, "because if I hadn't, Darius would have killed us both. You know that, Val."

He didn't reply, and she hesitated before asking almost timidly, "Why did you stop? Why didn't you make me…"

She trailed off, her face red with embarrassment.

His hand tightened into fists. "You belong to me. I will allow no other to see you."

He cursed under his breath and she jumped when he slammed his fist against the stone wall next to the fireplace.

Blood marred the stone where his skin tore but he didn't seem to notice as he stared into the flames.

"Go to sleep, Abigail," he commanded.

"I'm not sure I can," she whispered.

"I told you I won't fuck you. Unless you've changed your mind about letting me feed from you?"

"No. I haven't."

Despite how much she wanted him, despite the fact that her entire body was crying out for release from the lust that was throbbing through her and how she wanted to feel that sweet pain as his fangs slid into her skin, she couldn't allow him to bite her. She never wanted to be under anyone's control again.

"Then go to sleep," he bit out.

Her hands trembling badly, she turned down the covers of the bed. She could feel tears threatening and she blinked them back. She was dangerously close to breaking her promise and she was deeply ashamed of herself.

Val finally turned and looked at her. He took one look at her shaking body and her white face and snarled loudly. "Fuck!"

He was suddenly standing in front of her and she cried out in surprise when he pushed her onto the bed. He was kneeling on the floor, his hands pulling her legs apart and shoving her skirt up, before she had bounced to a stop on the bed.

He bent his head and licked the swollen, wet lips of her pussy. She cried out and spread her legs wide, exposing her hard and throbbing clit. He growled and buried his face into her, sucking and licking her clit as he shoved two fingers deep into her aching pussy.

She screamed as her orgasm roared through her, her entire body shaking and jerking against the bed as he continued to lick her clit. He thrust his fingers back and forth and she tried to scramble back, the pleasure suddenly too much. His other hand grabbed her hip and clamped down, pinning her to the bed as he licked and sucked on her clit. The pleasure was building inside of her again, hard bursts of lust exploding in her belly. She shouted his name and thrust her hips upwards as she came again, flooding his fingers and face with wetness.

She collapsed against the bed, her pulse roaring in her ears and her breath heaving in and out of her chest. Val pulled her skirt down and moved her gently to the far side of the bed. He stripped off his clothes and crawled in beside her.

His hand reached for the clasp of her top and she made a half-hearted attempt to stop him as he opened it and pulled it from her body.

"No," he growled. "I will no longer be denied what is mine. If I want your breasts bared, you will bare them. Do you understand?"

She murmured something he didn't hear but the tone was obvious. He leaned over her and sucked hard on one nipple while his fingers pulled the other, until her hips were arching against him and she moaned her assent.

He smiled with satisfaction, pulled the covers up around them and turned her on her side, spooning her tightly. She could feel his half-hard cock against her ass as he put his arm around her and cupped one naked breast.

"Go to sleep, little dove."

"Thank you, Val," she whispered.

She craned her head to look at him and he hesitated before kissing her on the mouth. "Go to sleep."

"SIENNA? WHERE ARE THE SLAVE QUARTERS?" ABIGAIL asked as they left the stone building. It was early the next morning and she had once again slipped out while Val was in his daysleep. She had accompanied Sienna to the prisoner house and had spent a few precious moments with Michael, Neil and Maria.

"Why?" Sienna asked.

"Lord Joven brought two other slaves with us and he asked me to look in on them." Abby smiled cheerfully at her.

"Oh. They are in the west end of the castle. I am on my way back to my room, I can take you there if you like." Sienna touched the small holes on her neck as she led Abigail back through the front doors of the stone castle. The brunette was pale and tired looking, and she yawned hugely as they walked through the wide, empty corridors.

"You were with Faren again last night?" Abby asked.

"Yes."

"Did he treat you well?"

"He did." Sienna smiled a little.

"Does the Lord Darius have parties like that every night?" Abby asked.

"No. Only on the nights of the games. If he did this every night, we would be drank dry in a matter of days. He may not have much mercy for his slaves, but even he realizes we need a day or two of rest in between feedings."

She gave a small, bitter laugh. "I will be off the menu this evening, even if Faren wishes to choose me again."

"How many slaves does Lord Darius keep?"

"Not as many as some vampires. He keeps enough to rotate us every couple of days. He enjoys having a variety of humans to quench his thirst and that of his men, but he does not enjoy having to feed us. Since he started his games, we are given even less food to compensate for the food he must give the slaves who fight."

"He does not seem to have many vampires in his household," Abby said.

Sienna shrugged. "He does not need many. The vampires he allows to live in his home are all very old and very powerful. It would not take many to protect his home against a threat. Besides, he has the shifters as well."

"Would the bear shifters really defend the vampires against other threats?" Abby asked. "I have never heard of shifters being loyal to a vampire before."

"Lord Darius believes they would. Whether that is true or not, I cannot say." Sienna pushed open a door and Abby followed her down another hallway.

"Why is it that you are given so much freedom to move about the castle while the vampires sleep?" Abby asked.

Sienna shrugged. "Perhaps because I am weak. They know I will not leave. I wouldn't survive a day in the forest. I have no skills with weapons and there are many creatures that lurk in the trees. Besides, the only way out is guarded by shifters."

She paused in the hallway and gave Abby a nervous look. "Shifters guard the slave quarters as well. These ones are not as easy-going as the shifters who guard the fighting slaves. Let me do the talking, all right?"

"All right."

Abigail followed Sienna around a corner. At the end of a hallway was another wooden door and two large men, both their faces heavily scarred, were staring silently at them. The women approached them and Sienna gave them a tentative smile.

"I am done with my chores for the day."

"Who is this one?" One of the men said.

"The Lord Joven's personal slave. He has two other slaves and he wishes for her to check on them."

"Does he now? Does that idiot Darius know?"

"I – I am not sure," Sienna stuttered.

"We are on strict orders not to let anyone pass who does not belong." The second man leaned forward and gave Abigail a long sniff, his nose twitching as he looked her up and down.

"My master is a special guest of the Lord Darius," she said. "I would hate to see how he would react if Lord Joven is denied what he wants."

"Are you threatening me?" The shifter asked.

"Of course not, my lord." Abby stared down at the floor. "I simply wish to spare you any unpleasant repercussions you may encounter if you deny me access."

He regarded her for a long silent moment as Abby kept her eyes on the floor between her feet. Finally, with a harsh grunt, he opened the door. Nodding at him, Abby followed Sienna down the hallway. The corridor was lined with doors, most of them shut and Sienna showed her to the final door on the right.

"The slaves will be in here." She smiled wearily at Abby and trudged back to her own room. Abigail watched until she had disappeared into the room before knocking on the door in front of her.

"Wesley? Evan? Open the door."

The door swung open almost immediately and Wesley stared with relief at her. "Abigail!"

She stepped into the room and Wesley shut the door before folding her into his embrace. He hugged her tightly for a few moments before kissing her cheek. "Are you okay?"

"Yes. Are you?" She asked as she hugged Evan.

"Fine. Starving, but fine," Evan grumbled. "They're not particularly fond of feeding the humans here."

Abigail squeezed his shoulder as Wesley led her to the

fireplace. She sat down in one of the chairs and looked around the room. It was very bare, with only one bed and a couple of chairs, and she gave the two men a look of dismay. "This is awful."

Wesley laughed as he sat down. "Believe me, I've slept in worse places."

He glanced at the door. "How did you get past the shifters? We have not been able to leave this room since the moment we arrived."

"I've made friends with one of the other slaves. She helped me get into the slave quarters."

"Are you – are you doing okay? Has the leech been behaving himself?" Wesley's gaze dropped to her neck and she nodded.

"I'm just fine, Wesley. I told you – Val will not hurt me."

"So, this Darius believes he is Joven?" Evan asked in a low voice.

"I am not sure that he is entirely convinced. Jaxen's assurance that he is Joven helped a little, but I believe that Darius is still suspicious. Although, that may just be his nature in general."

Wesley sighed angrily. "The leech needs to do a better job of convincing him."

"He is doing the best he can." Abigail frowned at him.

"Your continual defending of the leech is really starting to get on my nerves," Wesley said. "He's a monster and you would be wise to remember that."

"Enough, Wesley," Abigail replied. "Now is not the time to discuss this."

"I just think -"

"She's right," Evan interrupted as he raked his hand through his red hair. "Have you seen Michael? Does he live?"

Abigail smiled at him. "Yes, he does."

"Thank God," Wesley breathed.

"I have seen him and talked to him. He is doing well, all things considered." Abigail stared into the flames. "But we need to get him out of here. Darius uses him often during the games and although Michael is skilled, sooner or later the lack of food and his weariness will cost him his life."

"All right. So, let's make a plan," Evan said. "How heavily are the grounds guarded during the day?"

"Not very," Abigail replied. "Darius has remarkably few vampires on the property. Although Sienna says that the ones he does have are very old and very powerful. However, during the day, the security is quite lax. They have a shifter that guards the prison house, two shifters here in the slave quarters and maybe two or three at the front gates. It was difficult to tell."

"Good. So, we'll simply wait until the leeches are in their daysleep, take out the shifters, and leave," Evan said.

Wesley frowned at him. "We have no weapons, Evan. How do we take out the shifters?"

"Abby can do it."

"She has no weapons either."

"Val has his sword," Abby said. "I can use it."

"Abby can kill the shifters that guard us and then the three of us will rescue Michael and make our escape," Evan said.

"And what of Val and Jaxen?" Abby asked. "They cannot leave during the daylight hours."

Wesley sighed harshly. "Jaxen will be fine. He has been living with Darius for the last three months. He can simply slip away later that night."

"And Val? It will not take Darius long to realize that it was the three of us who released Michael and the other prisoners and -"

"The other prisoners?" Wesley interrupted. "We cannot take the others with us. It's too dangerous."

"We are not leaving them behind!" Abby snapped. "Not Neil or Maria and not the others. Once we are free of the estate, they can go their own way, but I will not leave any of them in those cells. And that includes the house slaves, as well. We give them the chance to leave with us."

"Abby -"

"No!" She stood and paced back and forth in the small room. "We are not leaving them, Wesley. I won't discuss it further."

He slumped back in the chair and stared moodily into the flames. "Of course. You're right, Abby. We can't leave them."

"I won't leave without Val either," Abby said.

Wesley's eyes widened and he nearly jumped out of his chair. He grabbed her shoulders and shook her. "Now you're being completely ridiculous."

"I am not." She pulled herself free and stared calmly at him. "If it weren't for Val, we wouldn't have even been able to get into Darius' estate."

Wesley snorted dismissively. "The only reason he's here is because he killed Joven. If he hadn't -"

"If he hadn't, I would most likely be firmly under Joven's spell," Abigail said. "I can deny it all I want but I would not have been able to stop Joven from biting me. Nor would I have been able to resist him once he had. Our plan was a desperate and foolish one born of our need to rescue Michael no matter what the cost. Val intercepting us and killing Joven was the best thing that could have happened. You know it, Wesley."

"Is it? You say he isn't biting you, but you won't leave the

135

leech behind. That does not speak of someone who isn't being controlled by the leech's bite."

She scowled at him. "I have told you repeatedly that Val isn't biting me. I'm not going to have this argument with you again. Either you believe me, or you don't. But for the record – I'm not leaving without Val because he's saved my life numerous times, and because he's one of the reasons we even have a chance at rescuing Michael and perhaps making it out alive."

"Abby - "

"No. There will be no discussion on this. I will not leave without Val. Nor do I think we should just leave."

"What are you talking about?" Wesley gave her a startled look.

"Once we've killed the shifters and released the prisoners, we'll kill Darius and the other leeches. If we don't, even if we manage to escape their clutches, Darius will simply start again with new humans. It'll be dangerous. The vampires sleep in rooms blocked from the sun. If they wake from their daysleep while we are in the room, we'll be in trouble."

"It takes a lot to wake them," Evan pointed out, "and we'll simply be very quiet." He grinned at her.

"If we miss even one," Wesley said, "it could kill all of us."

"We have Jaxen and we have Val." Abigail pointed out. "Besides, all of us have killed vampires when they were not in their daysleep."

"I do not like this," Wesley sighed. "It was never part of the plan to kill them all."

"I don't like it either, but we don't have a choice," Abby replied. "The odds that they would catch up to us in the forest when they woke and discovered their slaves missing is very high anyway. Besides, I didn't count on so few leeches living on Darius' estate. Now is our chance to end the games once and for all. We must kill them."

Wesley sighed. "When are we doing this?"

"In the next few days. The sooner we do this the better," Abby said. She leaned forward and pecked Wesley on the cheek before hugging Evan. "I need to go before the shifters become suspicious."

CHAPTER 12

Val sat by the fireplace and stared at the flickering flames. Abigail was sleeping in his bed and he sighed before adding another log to the fire. After tasting Abby's sweet cream last night, after seeing her lips wrapped around his cock, he was nearly desperate to take her. He clenched his fists and controlled both his desire and his blood lust with an almost painful ferocity. Every day he grew weaker. At this point he wasn't entirely sure he could even use the sword he wore around his waist. If he didn't feed soon he would be completely useless to Abby if there was trouble.

Violet crawled out from her bed on the windowsill. After stretching delicately, she flew to him. She sat on his shoulder and kissed his cheek before resting her head against his neck.

"I have no dried meat left for you, bug," he said. "I will have Abigail bring some food to you tonight, all right?"

She nodded and kissed him again as he returned to staring into the fire.

It would be nearly impossible to escape the grounds and feed on the forest animals without Darius discovering him.

He licked his lips and sighed again. Perhaps he could sneak to the barn and feed off one of the few horses Darius kept.

He snorted to himself and felt a thread of dismay at how far he had fallen. He had once drank from any human that caught his eye, and now he couldn't stomach the thought of feeding from anyone but Abigail. He was acting ridiculous, considering drinking from a horse rather than –

There was a soft knock on the door and Jaxen stepped into the room. He glanced at the sleeping Abigail before joining Val in front of the fireplace. He dropped into the chair across from him and studied Val closely.

"I know who you really are," he said.

Val stiffened. "I am no one."

"That isn't entirely true, is it, Valkyn?"

Val shot across the short distance, Violet tumbling from his shoulder, and grabbed the old vampire around the throat. He squeezed mercilessly as he glared at Jaxen. "How do you know that name, old man?"

Jaxen made a gurgling noise, his hands pulling at Val's, and Val released him with an angry shake before returning to his seat. He smoothed his hair back as Jaxen coughed quietly.

"Many years ago, I spent nearly a century in the north. It was my father's birthplace and I wanted to experience it for myself." Jaxen cleared his throat hoarsely. "At that time, your father was still a powerful and formidable King. There were many who shuddered at his name."

"With good reason. He was a cruel and unforgiving tyrant who ruled his people with bloodshed and without mercy," Val said. "And lower your voice. If she wakes and hears you speaking of this, I will kill you. Make no doubt about it. I am, after all, my father's son."

Jaxen gave him a nervous look before glancing over his shoulder at Abby. "So, she does not know that you are royalty and that you are the next in line for the throne? That your father, King Maridus, was responsible for saving our kind during the sickness?"

"No, she does not. And if you wish to keep your head firmly on your shoulders, it will remain that way."

"Before I joined Darius' estate, I kept up to date on news from the north. Do you know that even now, so many centuries later, your father still searches for you?"

"I'm aware," Val said. Violet had returned to his shoulder and she stroked his long hair soothingly.

"Did you know that he is ready to step down from the throne?"

Val laughed bitterly. "My father will never relinquish the throne while he still lives."

"That's not the rumour I've heard."

"It is nothing but rumour. Trust me, Jaxen. I know my father better than anyone."

Jaxen gave him a curious look. "I do not understand why you would not accept this gift. Your father is one of the most powerful vampires in the land. He has turned thousands of humans to vampires and yet, out of all of those he turned, he chose you as his son. He chose *you* to be the one to rule his people. Why would you walk away from that? You do not strike me as a coward."

"Watch your tongue," Val said. "Especially when you speak on matters you know nothing about."

"Then tell me," Jaxen replied. "Tell me why the vampire chosen to be the king's son would disappear instead of claiming what is rightfully his."

"It is no more my right, then yours," Val said. "This so-called line of royalty is a complete farce. My real father was nothing more than a baker. I grew up working in his shop, smelling of bread and yeast and always covered in flour.

My father was a good man, a kind man who wished that I would take over his business, but I longed for more. I wasn't satisfied being just a shop owner and when the war broke out between the humans, I immediately joined the battle. When King Maridus grew tired of the human's petty fighting and brought his army of vampires to wipe us out, I don't know why he spared my life. I was already dying when the vampires attacked. A sword had pierced my chest, and I was moments from death when the King turned me. He kept me by his side for over a century before declaring me his son. I – the son of a baker – was now the son of a king. It could have easily been any other man on that battlefield."

"He must have chosen you for a reason," Jaxen replied. "Even now, after two hundred years, he still searches for you."

Val snorted. "He does not search for me out of any type of fondness. He simply wishes to find me so that he can remove me of my head."

"Why?" Jaxen asked before taking another quick look at Abigail. "And why do you have such hatred for the vampire who gave you life?"

"You spoke of the sickness that the king saved his people from?"

"Yes. He discovered a cure just as we were on the verge of being wiped out."

"Yes, I am well aware of that," Val said. "The king was nearly frantic to find a cure and you can imagine his surprise that the key to our survival was living in his very home."

"You?" Jaxen gave him a surprised look.

Val shook his head. "No. I was dying from the sickness myself. It was one of the reasons the king was so anxious to find a cure. He had appointed me as the next ruler and, for whatever reason, was unwilling to accept that I would die, and he would be forced to choose another."

"Then who?"

"There was a young woman who lived in the palace. A vampire, not particularly pretty or special, and she spent her days cleaning the castle. At that point, there were so few left of us that we could no longer keep humans as slaves. There were not enough of us to keep them under control."

"I remember," Jaxen replied. "Do you remember the vampire in the south? Leanus was his name."

"I remember him well. He sought out every remaining healthy vampire in his city and urged them to band together. They went through the south, turning nearly every human they could find in an attempt to continue the vampire line."

"Fools," Jaxen snorted. "The humans they turned fell prey to the sickness more easily than those of us who were vampires for centuries. He accomplished nothing but angering the humans and leaving a trail of dead or dying vampires in his wake."

"My father had him killed," Val said.

Jaxen stared at him in surprise. "I had not heard that."

"It was kept quiet. Despite his obvious failure, there were many desperate vampires who believed it might work so the king kept his assassination a well-kept secret."

"Fascinating." Jaxen stared into the fire before turning back to Val. "Go on. You were saying about the girl."

"Her name was Karena." The glow of the flames high-lighted the paleness of his skin. "I loved her."

When Jaxen didn't reply, Val stared briefly at him before continuing. "We kept our love hidden, obviously. The son of the king in love with a chambermaid was not something my father would have tolerated."

He ignored Violet's soft petting. "When the sickness

finally descended upon the palace, I was one of the first to fall ill. The king grew frantic to save me, but I was dying just like the rest of them. The sores had covered my body and the blood I drank did not sustain me, no matter how healthy or well-fed the human was."

He glanced again at Abigail. She hadn't moved and he relaxed a little. "Most of the palace fell ill very quickly. But my Karena did not. She used to sneak in and visit me as I lay dying in my room. The illness had progressed to the point where I was throwing up any blood they tried to feed me. One night, after watching me vomit up the human blood, in desperation Karena cut her wrist and urged me to drink. I didn't want to, but I loved her and wanted to please her, so I drank. It was only a few mouthfuls, I was very weak, but it made her happy."

"What happened then?" Jaxen asked.

"In the morning, I was completely healed."

"Her blood – she was one of the immune," Jaxen whispered.

"Yes, she was. When she realized what she had done, Karena immediately went to my father. I begged her not to. Even then I knew what he was like, but she would not be stopped. She was very," a brief smile crossed Val's face, "stubborn. She told my father what she had done and brought me in to prove it to him. My father, who had fallen ill himself, was rather pleased, as you can imagine."

"Where is Karena now?"

"When my father realized that her blood was the key to healing the sickness, he had her drained dry" Val said.

"Why would he do that?" Jaxen asked. "It would have been more beneficial to him to keep her alive, to only drain her of a bit and allow her to feed and recover before - "

"He killed her because I loved her!" Val snarled. "I made

the mistake of letting him see my love for her. She is dead because of me! He couldn't stand the thought of his *son* being in love with a vampire like her, and so he drained her dry without considering the consequences of his actions."

"He is mad," Jaxen said with soft wonderment.

"You have no idea," Val said. "Once he realized his mistake, he began the search for other vampires who were immune. He believed that if Karena existed, there would be others who would too. And he was right. He found others and used them to save the vampire race."

"You left after that?" Jaxen asked.

"Yes. While he was busy hunting down the immune, I disappeared. I will never go back to the north and I will never take his place on the throne. He can choose another or let his kingdom fall. It matters not to me either way. He searches for me now only to kill me for my cowardice in leaving."

Jaxen took a deep breath. "If I recognize you, the odds are that there will be others within Darius' walls who recognize you too. You've put Abigail and the others in terrible danger by accompanying them here."

"Do you think I don't know that?" Val said. "I had no choice. Abigail was going to Darius' estate with or without me and I could not leave her to her fate. She is mine and I will destroy anyone who tries to take her from me."

His voice was rising. Jaxen made a shushing gesture with his hands before glancing nervously at Abby. "We must carry out our plan of rescue quickly. The sooner we can get you out of here, the better. I do not believe that Darius is completely convinced you are Joven."

"I know," Val said. "I will speak with Abigail about her plans for rescuing this Michael. I am sure she has something up her sleeve."

Jaxen grinned ruefully at him. "I have no doubt of it. She is quite remarkable, isn't she?"

"Yes, she is."

ABBY, HER FACE PALE AND HER EYES WIDE, STRUGGLED TO keep her breathing slow and even. She woke shortly after Jaxen entered the room. She had to stop herself from rising and going to Val when he had spoken of Karena. The pain in his voice had pierced her heart and she wanted desperately to soothe him. She forced herself to lie still and when she heard the sound of Jaxen rising, she closed her eyes and continued to feign sleep. Val did not want her to know of his love for Karena and she fought bitterly against the jealousy. He still loved Karena, she could hear it in his voice, and she was unprepared for the hurt that was flooding through her. She knew that Val desired her only for her blood, but to hear of his love for another was shattering her heart. She cursed herself inwardly. She was in love with Val. She could deny it all she wanted but it didn't make it any less true.

As Jaxen left the room, she stirred in the bed and yawned before sitting up and rubbing at her face. Val still sat in front of the fire and he didn't look at her as she slid out of the bed and crossed to him.

"Who was that?" She asked.

"Jaxen." He was still refusing to look at her and she blinked back the tears as Violet landed on her shoulder. She kissed the top of the pixie's head and sat in the chair across from him.

"What did he want?"

"He believes we should move quickly on our plan to rescue the others. I agree."

"I spoke with Wesley and Evan this morning."

He finally looked at her. "You did what?"

"I went to the slave quarters and spoke with Wesley and Evan," she repeated.

"Why would you be so foolish?" He snapped at her. "It is not safe for you to leave my side. Do you hear me?"

She just shrugged and stared into the fire. He gave her a curious look. Her face was pale and her usual defiant look to his rules had not appeared.

"Little dove? What is wrong?"

"Nothing," she said. "Darius is a fool. He leaves his home open to attack while he and the other leeches sleep. They're using bear shifters for protection but only a few."

"Shifters? Are you certain?" He asked.

"Yes. One guards the fighting slaves, two guard the slave quarters, and there are two, maybe three, who guard the entrance to his estate during the day. I will kill the shifters guarding the slave quarters and then Wesley, Evan and I will destroy the remaining shifters before freeing the slaves. Once Michael and the others are free, we will kill the leeches while they daysleep."

He gaped at her. "Have you gone mad? You think because you killed a bear shifter in the forest that you are capable of killing two? This plan is too dangerous, Abigail. And killing the leeches while they sleep? You do realize that we are capable of waking from our daysleep, do you not?"

"I'm aware of it. We'll be quiet."

"You'll be quiet?" He shook his head in disbelief. "This plan of yours is going to get us all killed."

"What would you suggest then?" She glared at him. "We cannot attack the leeches during the night! That will definitely get us killed."

"I – I realize that," he stuttered. "But this plan of you

taking on shifters on your own and then killing the vampires is not -"

"It is the best plan we have. I can take care of myself, Val. We can't leave Darius alive. You know that. If we do, he will only find more humans for his sick little games. We have to kill him. You can't really believe that we were coming here only to rescue Michael."

"Abigail -"

"Enough, Val! Until you can come up with a better plan, this is the one we're going with. I'll be fine."

"When are you planning your big rescue attempt?"

"In a few days."

"When?" He persisted.

"What does it matter?" She asked. "You will be in your daysleep and will have no part of it, remember?"

She stood abruptly and crossed the room to her bag. She brushed her hair with hard, angry strokes before staring at the shuttered window. "Once this is done, Val, we go our separate ways."

"No, we will not," he said.

"Yes." She refused to look at him. "I won't let you bite me and if you can't have my blood, what is the point of us remaining together?"

"You belong to me," he said.

"It doesn't matter how many times you say that, it doesn't make it true."

CHAPTER 13

"You are quiet tonight, Lord Joven. Not enjoying the games?" Darius asked.

It was two days later, and they were once again sitting in the arena. Three fights had already happened. Val had quickly grown tired of the crowd's incessant cheering, and the smell of the spilled blood was nearly impossible to ignore. Abigail was sitting on his lap and he was studying the faint pulse in her neck when Darius spoke to him.

He forced himself to smile at the vampire. "Not at all. Simply wondering when we are going to discuss my part in this new empire of yours."

"All in good time, my dear Joven, all in good time. Are you not enjoying my hospitality? Do you not find the bed comfortable enough? Or perhaps your slave is not nearly enough for you. You're looking a little peaked these past few days. I'd be happy to find you another to feed from."

"The room is quite comfortable, and my slave is more than enough, thank you."

Faren leaned forward as the gates opened and the

vampires led out the first opponent in the final game. "That's a big one."

"Yes, she is the sister of the woman you saw the first night," Tavien replied. "She is not as deadly as her sister, but she gets the job done."

He frowned as the second opponent was brought out. "Although I fear this will be a short fight."

Val clamped his hand down on Abigail's wrist as she gasped sharply. Maria, looking small and fragile, was standing in the middle of the arena. She lifted her head defiantly and stared at the crowd as the vampire handed her a sword.

"No," Abby breathed as the vampires handed Dalia her own sword and quickly left the arena. Darius was already standing, and Abby moaned as he waved his hand at the two women.

"Begin!"

A grin crossing her wide face, Dalia lifted her sword as Maria did the same. Abby watched in horror as the larger woman began to stalk Maria. Her face bloodless, Maria gripped the sword grimly and managed to keep hold of it when Dalia struck it with her own.

The heavier woman was toying with her, laughing loudly as Maria struck determinedly at her with the sword, and the crowd booed heavily.

"Finish her!" Someone shouted.

Dalia shrugged and, with surprising quickness for her size, struck out with her sword. Maria's sword went flying across the arena and the smaller woman was knocked onto her back when Dalia delivered a hard blow to her stomach with the handle of her sword. Coughing and gagging, Maria dragged herself backward as Dalia stalked forward.

"God, this one is pathetic," Darius said with disgust. "It's not even a fight. I swear, Tavien, if you do not do a better job of -"

He was cut off by Val's loud yelp of surprise. Abigail had bitten him hard on the hand and when he released her wrist, she leaped from his lap and vaulted over the low stone wall in front of them. As she dashed across the arena, Val cursed and jumped to his feet. Before he could follow her, Darius reached out and gripped his shoulder.

"Remain where you are, Lord Joven, or I will have my men kill her immediately."

Dalia stood over Maria and raised her sword.

"Sorry about this," she said cheerfully.

She thrust her sword downward and gasped in surprise when it was blocked by Maria's sword. She stepped back and stared at the woman holding the sword and standing protectively over Maria.

"I know you," she said.

Without speaking, Abigail attacked her. Dalia flinched back and just barely got her sword up in time to protect herself. She backed away and grinned at Abigail. "Do you believe you can beat me?"

Abigail raised her sword and Dalia's grin widened. "Then let me see you try."

She lunged at Abigail, swinging her sword in a wide arc. Abby blocked it and danced away. The roaring of the crowd had faded away and she could hear nothing but the sound of her own heartbeat. As Dalia attacked her again, she parried the blow easily and, as their swords clashed repeatedly, she studied the way the big woman moved.

Compared to vampires, Dalia's attack was almost ridiculously slow and, unable to ignore how good it felt to have a sword in her hand again, Abby toyed with the woman for nearly five minutes. Finally, when Dalia's face was bright red and she was panting heavily, Abigail sliced the top of her arm.

Dalia dropped her sword with a bellow of pain and rage and glared at Abigail before lunging forward. Abby side-stepped her and stuck her foot out. Caught in her forward momentum, Dalia tripped over her foot and fell to the dirt.

She rolled onto her back, clutching at her arm, as Abigail kicked her sword away before placing the tip of her own sword against Dalia's chest. Snorting and breathing like an angry bear, Dalia stared up at her. Abby could see no fear in the woman's eyes and she felt a sliver of admiration go through her.

"Do you yield?" She asked.

The crowd began to chant. "Finish her! Finish her! Finish her!"

Abby stared at the vampires in the arena. They were standing on their feet and screaming, and she shook her head in disgust before her gaze landed on Val. Anger was written all over his face and she felt a ripple of hurt when he deliberately looked away from her.

She turned back to Dalia. "Do you yield?"

"Finish me and be done with it!" Dalia spat at her.

"I'm not going to kill you," Abby said.

She backed away before turning and hurrying to Maria. The crowd shrieked their disapproval as the smaller woman stared wide-eyed at her.

"Abby, what have you done?" She whispered.

"Maria, I -"

Maria's gaze flickered over her shoulder and her eyes widened in horror. "Look out!"

Abby whirled around. Dalia, her eyes wild and her sword raised high in the air, was nearly upon her. Without stopping to think about it, Abby thrust her sword into Dalia's chest.

The woman grunted loudly and looked down at the sword embedded into her flesh.

"Bitch," she wheezed.

Blood ran from her mouth and with a small wince, Abby yanked her sword free.

Dalia collapsed to her knees on the ground, her mouth opening and closing like a fish gulping for air, before her eyes rolled up in her head and she fell face down into the dirt.

The vampires screamed in response and Abby stared at them with undisguised disgust. Behind her, Maria made a noise of pain. She turned to see a vampire holding Maria's arm behind her back. He dragged her out of the arena as two others approached Abby.

She gave them a warning look. "Unless you want to die in front of this crowd, I would suggest you stand back."

They grinned at each other and stepped closer.

She sighed wearily. "Very well, then."

She raised her sword into fighting position as the crowd quieted.

"Abigail!"

Val's voice, thick with anger, rang out across the arena.

Abby stiffened and turned to look at him. He was standing in front of the low stone wall and he held his hand out impatiently. "Come to me. Now."

She smiled at the vampires who were inching toward her. "Another time, perhaps."

She dropped her sword and jogged back to Val. He lifted her over the stone wall, setting her roughly on her feet, and took her wrist in a firm grip as Darius eyed them both.

"You did not tell me that your slave was an accomplished fighter, Lord Joven."

"Believe me, Lord Darius, I am as surprised as you," Val replied.

Darius cocked his head at Abigail. "Why did you save that woman? Who is she?"

"I do not know, my lord," Abigail said. "I simply wanted to grant your wish for a fair fight. Is that not what you were looking for?"

"I suppose it was," Darius said. He turned to Val. "I will buy this slave from you for a thousand gold pieces."

"That is very generous of you but I'm afraid I must decline," Val said.

Darius snorted with impatience. "Fine. I will lower my cut of your profits in exchange for her."

"Again, I regretfully decline."

"Have you gone mad, Lord Joven?" Tavien said. "Do you understand the magnitude of this offer? Is the woman really worth it?"

Val didn't reply, and Darius shook his head. "Do not decline my offer so quickly, Lord Joven. Take a day or two to consider it."

He swept past them and, after a moment, the others followed.

"WHAT WERE YOU THINKING, ABIGAIL?" VAL TURNED ON her the moment they entered their room.

She glared at him. "You can't honestly believe that I was going to sit there and watch Maria die."

He raked his hand through his long hair before pacing the room. "Do you have any idea what you've done? Darius will stop at nothing to take you as his own. Do you get that?"

"I couldn't watch her die! Do you get that?"

"At the cost of your own freedom? Maybe even your life?"

He continued to pace as Violet buzzed anxiously around them.

Abigail took a deep breath. "I know what I did was stupid, but I won't apologize for saving Maria's life. Christ, Val, did you want to see her die?"

He scowled at her. "Of course, I didn't. Your continual belief that I am a cold-hearted monster is starting to wear on me."

"I don't think that," she said. "I just – I think your need for my blood has blinded you to the needs of your friends. Neil and Maria are our friends. I'm not just here for Michael."

He stood in front of the fire and stared into it as she approached him and patted his back timidly. "You need to eat, Val. It's been days and you're growing weak. I can see it and so can Darius."

He didn't reply, and she hesitated briefly. "I – I think you should feed from another slave tonight. It will lessen Darius' suspicion and restore your strength."

He swung around and stared angrily at her. "Is that what you want, little dove? Do you want to watch me feed from another woman? To fuck her?"

"You – you don't have to sleep with her," Abigail whispered.

"So, you want me to feed from another and fuck you. Is that right?"

"I didn't say that."

"I won't feed from a slave without fucking her, little dove. She would beg me to fuck her and I am not so cruel as to deny her what she needs."

"But I am?" Abigail said.

He reached out and yanked her against his hard body. He cupped her neck, holding her by the collar as his gaze dropped to her mouth. "Do you want me to feed from another?"

"No," she said, "I do not. But it doesn't mean I want you withering away, either."

He snorted. "I am not nearly as weak as you believe me to be, Abigail."

He stared hungrily at her breasts. She could feel his erection pushing against her and she swallowed hard, trying to ignore the ripple of lust that went through her.

"Val, I -"

He released her abruptly and stepped away, turning his back to her and staring into the fire again. "Enough. Leave me alone until we are back downstairs and must continue our charade again."

Violet landed on her shoulder and blinking back tears, Abigail hurried to the window. She stared out into the darkness as Violet stroked her hair and kissed her neck.

ABIGAIL PAUSED AS SHE WALKED DOWN THE HALLWAY. SHE could see the common room below them and she groaned inwardly. The festivities had already begun, and the vampires were feeding and fucking their slaves with unrestrained hunger.

Faren, his eyes closed in bliss, was reclining on a chaise as Sienna sucked his cock enthusiastically. Another slave, this one a sleek blonde, kissed and licked his chest. As she watched he tugged her upward and sank his fangs deep into her throat. The girl shuddered with ecstasy and a soft moan slipped from Abigail's lips.

Val stepped closer and pressed himself against her back. His cock was hard against her ass and another moan slipped out as he reached around her and cupped her breasts. He kneaded them as her back arched helplessly.

"Do you want me to fuck you, little dove?"

"You know I do." She whispered. She continued to watch the orgy below them, at the naked twisting, writhing bodies of the vampires and the humans, and felt a deep aching throb that only Val could take care of.

He reached for the clasp of her top. She didn't try and stop him as he popped it open and pulled it from her upper body. He dropped it to the floor and cupped her naked breasts, pulling firmly on her hard nipples. She moaned and reached behind her to rub at his cock.

She didn't care that the people below them could see her if they raised their heads. She didn't care that anyone who walked down the hallway would see the way she was rubbing herself against Val. What she wanted - what she needed - was Val's cock inside of her, and she could have cried with the knowledge that she would be denied again.

Despite knowing he would stop, that this wouldn't end with him fucking her the way she so desperately needed, she leaned back against him and arched her back again, pushing her breasts into his hands. He stared over her shoulder at her breasts as he pulled and rubbed her swollen and throbbing nipples.

"Does that feel good, little dove?"

"Yes," she moaned.

He pulled the back of her skirt up and she widened her thighs as he unbuttoned his pants and then pushed his erect cock between her ass cheeks. He rubbed it up and down and she ground her ass against him until he moaned.

"You win, Abigail," he breathed into her ear.

She gave him an uncertain look. An odd combination of

anger and lust was crossing his features and he shook his head before pushing her head roughly forward.

"I won't feed from you."

"You don't have to do this," she said. "You don't have to
-"

She cried out when he shoved his cock deep into her soaking wet pussy. After days of being denied, her pussy gripped him eagerly, sucking him deep into her body and holding him there as he panted harshly into her ear.

"I've missed your tight pussy, little dove," he muttered. "It clings to me so tightly, I can barely stop from coming."

"Please," she whispered.

He was deep inside of her but not moving. When she tried to thrust back against him, he cupped her throat and held her firmly. His fingers traced the collar around her neck as she moaned her need.

"Do you like wearing my collar, Abigail? Does it please you to know that it marks you as mine?" He whispered before moving roughly in and out.

She cried out with pleasure and pushed back against him desperately when he stopped again. "Does it? Tell me the truth."

"Yes!" She cried. "Please!"

"You're mine. Say it!" He demanded.

She shook her head, her dark hair brushing against his chest, and he reached around and cupped her pussy. His fingers found her swollen clit easily and he stroked it before turning her head and kissing her hard on the mouth. She sucked eagerly at his tongue, her hands rising to tug on her hard nipples, and he made his own groan of pleasure.

He stilled his fingers against her and tore his mouth from hers. She made a gasping whine of need. "Please don't stop."

"Tell me what I want to hear, little dove." He kissed the line of her jaw as she moaned and wiggled against him.

"Tell me and I'll give you the relief you need." He was nearly frantic with the need to come and Abigail's wet pussy was driving him insane. He gritted his teeth and waited. He needed to hear her say it, he needed to know that she was his and –

"I'm yours!" She suddenly cried and with a loud growl he plunged in and out of her as his fingers pulled on her clit.

She threw her hand over her mouth and screamed as she came uncontrollably around his cock. Her pussy, squeezing and tightening in rhythmic surges, drove him over the edge and he threw his head back and climaxed.

His fangs lengthened. He moaned as he studied the smooth, pale flesh of Abigail's shoulder. He could bite her now, he could take from her what he needed, and she wouldn't be able to stop him. His thirst for her was nearly out of control. With a strangled curse, he pulled out of her and staggered a few feet away. He rested his hand on the wall in front of him, breathing heavily as his pulse roared in his ears and his body shrieked at him to feed.

Abigail, her legs trembling badly, quickly slipped into her top. She closed the front clasp and waited patiently as Val leaned against the wall. She wanted to go to him, but she knew if she went near him now, he would feed from her. She kept her distance and waited.

After nearly five minutes, Val buttoned his pants and turned around. His face was even paler than normal. Guilt flooded through her when he wiped his mouth harshly and gave her an almost desperate look of hunger.

"Are you all right?" She whispered.

He closed his eyes and took several deep breaths. "Go back to our room."

"What? No, I -"

She reached out to touch his arm and he pulled back from her.

"Do not touch me, little dove!"

"I'm sorry," she whispered.

"Go back to our room. I only have so much control and it's not wise for you to be around me right now."

She gave him a guilty look and he sighed. "Go, Abigail."

"Will you feed from another?"

"Please, Abigail!" He said. "You must leave now!"

He took a step toward her, his face twisting, and she turned and fled. He slammed his fist into the stone wall, hissing at the pain, before wiping the blood from his hand and walking down the stairs to the common room.

Tavien, his eyes gleaming, stepped out of the shadows. He stared at Val, before abruptly turning and striding away.

CHAPTER 14

"**M**y lord. I must speak with you." Tavien spoke urgently into Darius' ear. Darius frowned irritably at him.

"I'm busy."

"It is of great importance."

"Then speak, Tavien," Darius said.

"Not here, my lord." Tavien glanced around the common room.

Darius pushed the woman from his cock. She gave him a disappointed look and he patted her head like she was a dog and buttoned his pants before standing. "This had better be good, Tavien."

He followed him out of the common room and down the hallway to Tavien's room. There was a large book sitting on the bed and Tavien leafed through it quickly.

"I was in the library and -"

"I have a library?"

"Yes," Tavien replied with an edge of impatience in his voice. "I knew I had seen Lord Joven somewhere before and -"

161

"How long have I had a library? How many books are in there?" Darius asked.

"Lord Darius! Please, pay attention."

Darius sighed and glanced at the door. "I cannot ignore my guests, Tavien."

"I know. But you must look at this." He nearly shoved the book into Darius' hands and pointed to the page in front of him. There was an ink drawing of a young man standing next to a larger, older man.

Darius blinked in surprise and studied the older man. "Is that the king of the north? Maridus?"

"Yes. But look at the man standing next to him."

Darius squinted at the picture. "What of him?"

"What do you mean, what of him?" Tavien snapped.

Darius' nostrils flared. "Watch your tongue, Tavien."

"My apologies, my lord. It's just – I believe that man, the king's son, is the very man who pretends to be Lord Joven."

Darius gave the picture a cursory look before glancing at the door again. "There is a resemblance."

"More than a resemblance, my lord," Tavien insisted.

Darius gave him a curious look. "How often do you go to the library and read, Tavien? And when do you do it?"

"My lord," Tavien said with barely restrained impatience, "do you not see that this man in the picture is, in fact, Lord Joven?"

Darius narrowed his eyes and read the wording below it. "You're telling me that this Valkyn is masquerading as Joven?"

"I am."

Darius scoffed loudly. "Why would the king's son be here? Hmm? The idea is ridiculous. Although I am not entirely sure that he is Joven, I am most certain he is not the future king of the north."

"The king's son disappeared many years ago. Some say he died of the sickness but there are many who believed he sought to escape the pressures his father put on him," Tavien said.

"How do you know this?"

"I read, Lord Darius, remember?"

Darius studied him. "You really do believe he is this man, don't you?"

"I do."

Darius examined the picture more closely and Tavien nodded eagerly when he said, "He does bear a remarkable resemblance to him."

"There is something else, Lord Darius."

"What?"

"Earlier, I was in the hallway when this Joven and his slave girl walked by. They fucked in the hallway above the common room."

"So? That is hardly surprising." Darius frowned.

"He did not feed from her."

"What do you mean?"

"He fucked her but didn't feed from her. Didn't even give her a friendly love bite. In fact, it seemed he was doing everything he could *not* to bite her. I have never seen a vampire fuck a human without feeding from them. Have you?"

"No, I have not," Darius said.

He shut the book with a snap and handed it to Tavien. "I believe it's time we had a talk with Lord Joven. Don't you, Tavien?"

"Yes, my lord."

"Good. Have my men meet me here in five minutes. Make sure Joven stays in the common room."

"Faren! Faren!"

"What?" Faren opened his eyes and stared at Val. "What is your problem?"

"Something is going on."

"What do you mean?"

"I mean, we're the only ones left in the room."

Faren sat up. Sienna had fallen asleep against his chest and she made a soft whimper of disapproval when he moved her to the chaise beside him before covering her face with her hand.

Faren rubbed her ass as he stared around the common one. "We're not the only ones."

"With the exception of Jaxen," Val pointed to the old vampire who was reclining on a couch and kissing a young man lazily, "the rest are all slaves."

A look of alarm crossed Faren's face. "Well, this can't be good."

"You think?" Val said. He raised his voice and called to Jaxen. The vampire pulled away from his slave and walked over.

"What is it, Lord Joven?"

"Where are Darius and the others?"

Jaxen stared around the room before blinking in surprise. "I – I do not know."

"We need to go," Val said. "We need to -"

He broke off as Darius, Tavien and his men entered the common room.

"Lord Joven! Enjoying yourself this evening?" He asked.

"Very much so. But it grows late, and I am tired. I believe I will say my goodbye and retire for the day." Val rose from his chair as Darius held up his hand.

"Of course, of course. We will let you return to your room in a moment."

He clapped his hands loudly. "Slaves – get out! Now!"

The slaves, most of them groggy or weak from being fed on, stumbled to their feet and hurried from the room.

Val's hand went to his sword and he gripped the handle as Darius' men elbowed Faren and Jaxen back and surrounded him in a tight circle.

"What is going on, Lord Darius?" Jaxen asked.

"You're looking very pale, Lord Joven. Are you sure you're getting enough to eat?" Darius asked.

Val didn't reply and Jaxen gave Darius a troubled look. "Lord Darius, please, what - "

"It occurred to me today that I really only have your word that the man standing in front of me is Joven." Darius arched his eyebrows at Jaxen.

"I can assure you, Lord Darius, that this is Joven," Jaxen said. "I have known him for many years."

"Yes, but who knows how long a man is willing to pretend to be another?" Darius said. "Why, if they were desperate enough, they might go years impersonating someone."

He turned his gaze to Jaxen again. "Or, someone who I believed to be a trusted friend is lying to me."

"I am not," Jaxen said. "He is the Lord Joven and he -"

"You spent time in the north, did you not, Jaxen?" Darius said.

Jaxen nodded. "I did. Many years ago."

"I suppose you remember the king of the north."

"Yes, Maridus is his name."

"Lord Joven bears a remarkable resemblance to the king's son. What was his name? Do you remember?"

Jaxen shrugged. "No, my lord, I do not. Besides, the king's son is dead. The sickness took him, along with many others, in the royal castle. From what I remember, King

Maridus himself grew ill and it was only his discovery of the immune that kept him from dying."

"The king's son is dead? That is not the rumour I have heard. It is interesting that I would have someone in my home who resembles him so closely."

Jaxen shrugged again. "Many people have similar features, my lord."

"That is true," Darius acknowledged. "But you must understand if I do not take your word for it."

He made a small, almost imperceptible nod, and Val's eyes widened before he turned quickly. He was reaching for his sword when the vampires behind him threw the long silver chains against his body. Already weak from hunger, Val hissed in pain and collapsed to the floor as Faren gave a startled yell.

"Hey! What is the meaning of this? You cannot -"

He held his hands up and backed up a step as another vampire held a sword to his throat.

"Stay quiet, please," Darius said. He watched as his men threw more chains onto Val's body. Smoke was beginning to rise into the air, and he wrinkled his nose at the smell of burning flesh before holding his hand out.

The vampire closest to him handed him a pair of leather gloves and he slipped them on before squatting next to Val. He traced his cheek with one finger and Val snarled at him, his fangs glistening in the light of the candles, before jerking his head away.

"I can't imagine how badly this hurts." Darius tugged on one of the chains before holding his hand out. "I'll admit, I'm impressed that you're not screaming."

Val hissed again as Tavien placed a silver rod in Darius' hand. It had been sharpened to a deadly point at one end and

Darius poked it against Val's face. It left a burn mark and he grinned before slapping Val across the face.

"You and I are going to have a little talk, Joven. If you can convince me that you are in fact who you say you are, I will let you live. I won't lie – this is going to be excruciating."

He laughed and Faren and Jaxen both winced when he slammed the silver rod against Val's face. His cheekbone broke with a loud crack and Val made a muffled groan of pain before falling silent.

"Let's begin, shall we?" Darius smiled.

"I LOVE HIM, VIOLET, AND AT THIS VERY MOMENT HE IS probably feeding from and fucking another," Abigail said. She was sitting by the window, staring out into the darkness as Violet sat cross-legged in her basket and watched her closely.

"He's feeding from another because I forced him to it by not allowing him to feed from me. And for what reason? I know that I love him, I know that I would want him desperately regardless of whether he was taking my blood." Abigail ran her fingers through her long, dark hair. "I am a fool, little one."

Violet gave her a look of sorrow before reaching out and patting her hand.

"I was so determined to prove to him that I wasn't the same scared, fat, Abby who didn't need him or anyone else that I've driven him away."

She swiped at the tears that were starting to slide down her face. "I know he doesn't love me and that he still loves this Karena woman, but even still – I can't stop loving him."

The door to the bedroom flew open and Violet dove into the basket as Faren rushed into the room. He was wild-eyed, and he gave Abigail a look of panic.

"Abigail! You must come quickly!"

"Faren? What is wrong?" Abigail jumped to her feet and crossed the room. "What's happened? Why are you -"

"He is dying, Abigail! Move!"

Adrenaline flooded through her veins and, without another word, she followed Faren. He led her to the common room, and she stared horrified at the man lying on the floor. His body was bloodied and burned, and his face had been beaten until it was nearly unrecognizable.

She fell to her knees beside him and touched his face. He made a soft groan of pain and she raised her terrified gaze to Darius. "What have you done?"

"We needed to be certain he was Joven. You understand," Darius replied.

She stared at the silver rod in his hands and at the silver chains lying next to Val's body. "So you burned him with silver? What kind of monster are you?"

"Oh, come now. No need for such hysterics, my pet. The good news is – he did a remarkable job of convincing us he was Joven. I know of many men who would have admitted to almost anything just to stop the pain. Your master has not faltered in his insistence that he is Joven."

"Besides, he will be fine," Darius continued cheerfully. "A bit of your blood and he'll be right as rain. Go on – let him feed. Unless," he cocked his head at her, "there is a reason you will not give him your blood?"

Abigail quickly swept her hair back. She leaned over Val and kissed him on his bruised and swollen mouth.

"My lord, open your eyes."

He didn't respond, and fear shot through her. She shook him roughly and he groaned again. "Look at me, my love!"

His eyelids fluttered open and he stared wearily at her. "Little dove?"

"That's right. You must feed, my love. Go on." She pressed her throat against his mouth. When he didn't bite her, she took his hand and squeezed it.

"Please, I want you to feed from me. Please," she whispered.

For a moment there was nothing and then her back arched and she gave a soft cry as Val's fangs sunk into her neck. He drank greedily, and she closed her eyes and squeezed his hand again.

The smell of burned flesh was receding, and her eyes flew open when Val suddenly flipped her onto her back. His flesh and bones were beginning to heal, and he gave her a brief, haunted look before bending his mouth to her neck and drinking again.

She arched her back, feeling lust and need flowing through her as Val drank deeply. When his hand cupped her breast, she moaned and clutched at his waist. Her desire was ebbing away as her body grew weak, and she pushed tiredly at Val's chest. He growled and pinned her hands down before continuing to drink.

"Please," she whispered.

———

VAL, HIS PULSE POUNDING IN HIS EARS, BARELY HEARD HER whispered plea. Abigail's blood was flowing through his veins and tasting sweeter and thicker than he remembered. As it healed his body he sucked eagerly at her neck. He wanted to fuck her senseless, he wanted to bury himself in her body until she was screaming his name. He squeezed her breast again and when she didn't respond, panic fluttered through him. He tore his mouth away from her neck and stared at her face. She was very pale, and her eyes were closed. He bit back his cry of worry and stroked her face.

"Little dove, open your eyes."

She blinked hazily at him before closing her eyes again. "You're better."

Val rose to his feet. He was nearly vibrating with power from Abigail's blood and he studied the vampires in the room. He wanted to kill them all, he wanted to rip their heads from their bodies and watch as they burned and –

"Feeling better, Lord Joven?" Darius inquired.

Val forced himself to relax. He could not kill all of them and protect Abigail at the same time. She was unconscious on the floor and, ignoring Darius and the others, he lifted her and carried her out of the room.

CHAPTER 15

Abigail stretched and rubbed at her face before opening her eyes. Val's face was directly above hers and she gave a startled little yelp as her heart jumped in her chest.

"Jesus, Val!" She rubbed at her chest. "Don't do that."

"How do you feel?" He asked anxiously.

"I'm tired but I'll be fine. What time is it?"

"It's early evening."

She blinked at him in surprise. "I slept all day?"

"Yes."

"Well, shit." It had been her plan to kill the shifters guarding Wesley and Evan this morning and put into motion their rescue. She'd fucked up. Of course, she hadn't planned on having to save Val's life last night. She sat up and leaned against the headboard of the bed as Val left her side and returned with a tray of food.

"You must eat, little dove. Eat lots. You need to regain your strength."

She needed no urging. She was starving and she ate ravenously as Val sat on the bed beside her. She ate her fill and then covered her mouth when she burped.

"Sorry." She flushed as a small smile crossed Val's face.

"Drink." He handed her a large glass of water and she drank all of it.

Violet hovered beside her and Abby smiled at the pixie. "I'm fine, little one. Just tired."

"I'm sorry, little dove. I should not have taken so much from you," Val said.

"You had no choice."

He reached out and stroked her dark hair. "Why did you let me feed from you?"

"Because you were dying, and because I love you."

He gaped at her. "Little dove, you – you do not love me. I am not who you believe me to be and -"

"I was awake when you and Jaxen were speaking in our room. I know exactly who you are and the loss you have suffered."

Val felt like the breath had been sucked out of him. He knew he looked ridiculous simply staring at her with his mouth wide open, but he couldn't think of a response.

She crawled out from under the covers, nestling her body into his and wrapping her arms around his neck. She kissed his throat and smoothed his hair back before whispering into his ear. "I know you do not love me and never will. I know your heart will always belong to Karena, and I'm sorry that your father took her from you in such a terrible way."

"Abigail - "

She shook her head and kissed his mouth. "It's all right. You care for me deeply, I know that. It's good enough."

She slipped her hand inside his shirt and rubbed his hard chest. "Make love to me, Val. I need you." She kissed his neck again, licking and sucking lightly as she stroked his warm skin.

Val stared blankly at the wall in front of them. He was reeling from her admission of love and he barely felt her gentle touch. His mind kept returning to her words, kept hearing the steady sound of her voice and the look of surety in her gaze when she said she loved him.

She loved him.

Despite what he was, what he had done, she loved him.

He had insulted her, had nearly killed her twice from drinking her blood, and acted like a spoiled, jealous child whenever anyone looked at her, and she still loved him.

"Val?"

"Yes?" He croaked.

"Are you okay? Your heart is really pounding." She traced her fingers over his chest and he captured her hand before bringing it to his lips.

"Your touch does that to me, little dove," he whispered.

She smiled before kissing him on the mouth. "I need you."

"I need you too," he replied. He cupped her breast, stroking her nipple gently with his fingers until it hardened. She squirmed closer until she was straddling him on the bed.

"You should rest more," he said but his hand was already slipping beneath her short skirt.

"I'll rest after. Oh!" She gasped as Val rubbed her pussy.

"Are you sure, my dove?" He groaned. "I do not want - "

There was a loud knocking on the door and Abby jerked in his arms when it opened and Tavien stepped into the room.

"Forgive me, Lord Joven. I did not mean to interrupt."

"You are, so get out," Val said.

"Of course." He smiled benignly at him. "But first, a gift from Lord Darius. As an apology for last evening."

He reached into the hallway and pulled a young woman into the room. She was short and slender with curly blonde hair that brushed her shoulders and she was dressed similarly to Abby in a tiny skirt and see through top. Her eyes were a light green. They were wide and frightened looking, and Abby could see the shine of tears in them.

She made a soft moan of terror when Tavien tugged lightly on her curly locks. "Lord Darius asks that you accept his apology and take this slave as a gift."

"No," Val said.

Tavien frowned at him before rubbing at the birthmark on his cheek. "You would deny your host's very generous gift? The girl is young and untouched. She has a timid nature and will train easily as your pet."

He stroked the woman's face and when she twitched away from him, he struck her harshly across the cheek. She cried out and stumbled into the wall as Abby slid from Val's lap. He caught her by the arm, and she gave him an impatient look that he ignored.

"I have no need for a second pet," Val said. "Tell Lord Darius I am," he paused and gave Tavien a sarcastic look, "touched by his eagerness to make amends but that the woman is unnecessary."

Tavien shrugged before grabbing the woman's arm and squeezing it. "Very well. I will inform him of your decision. Come, girl." He grinned down at her and the woman made another moan of terror at the sight of his fangs. "It seems it will be my bed you warm tonight."

"My lord?" Abby stroked Val's arm in a conciliatory manner. "It would please me greatly if you took the woman."

He frowned and she gave him a sweet look. "Please, my lord."

He stared silently at her for a moment before nodding. "Very well."

A look of disappointment flickered across Tavien's face, but he dropped the woman's arm and pushed her further into the room. "Will you be joining us in the common room this evening, Lord Joven?"

"I have not decided yet," Val said. "I'm sure Darius will understand why."

Tavien gave him a brittle smile before leaving the room. He closed the door behind him and the woman pressed her back against the door and stared with fright at Val.

"What are you doing, Abigail?" Val asked. "I do not need another pet."

"Tavien is cruel. I couldn't leave her with him." She scowled at him as he sighed and walked toward the woman still cowering against the door.

The woman held her trembling hands up and began to cry. "Please don't hurt me."

He rolled his eyes as Abby pushed past him. She smiled at the girl. "It's all right. No one in this room will hurt you. I promise."

The woman stared at the holes in Abigail's neck as more tears slid down her cheeks. "Please don't let him bite me."

"He won't," Abigail soothed. She stepped a little closer and held her arms out. "Come here, honey. You're safe."

With another frightened glance at Val, the girl stepped into Abigail's embrace and hugged her. She buried her face in Abby's neck and sobbed.

"Shh, don't cry. It'll be okay." Abby stroked her hair and rubbed her back as Val rolled his eyes again and stalked over to the fireplace. He sat down and closed his eyes as Abby tugged the girl back.

"What's your name, honey?"

"Sara."

"That's a pretty name. How old are you?"

"T-twenty," she stuttered. "Please, don't let him bite me."

Val snorted loudly and, without opening his eyes, said, "The girl is a frightened mouse. She won't last a week on her own, and once we leave here I am not keeping her. You should have given her to Tavien. At least then she would have a roof over her head and food in her belly."

"Enough, my lord," Abigail said.

She wiped at the tears on Sara's face. "Don't pay any attention to him. His bark is worse than his bite. Trust me."

The girl's face paled even further, and Abby groaned. "No, no – it's just a saying. I'm sorry, I didn't mean that he's going to bite you. He won't. Please believe me."

She tugged the woman toward the bed and urged her to sit down before sitting next to her. She took her hand and squeezed it. "My name is Abigail and that is," she paused, "Lord Joven."

"It – it is nice to meet you," Sara said. Her eyes kept flickering to Abby's throat and Abby touched the holes delicately before smiling at her.

"He feeds from me because I want him to. You do not, so he won't. Do you understand?"

"Yes."

"Good. Now, do you have any family?"

"No. I had an older brother, but he was killed by Darius' men when they took our village." She made a watery gasping sob and Abby rubbed her slender arms.

"I'm sorry for your loss. I know you are frightened and I know - "

Sara inhaled sharply when Violet poked her head out from Abby's hair and stared curiously at her.

"You – you have a pixie!"

"Yes. Her name is Violet. She doesn't speak," Abby replied.

Violet flew to Val and landed on his knee. He didn't open his eyes and she climbed up his body before pinching his lower lip.

"Enough, bug," he growled.

She pinched his lip again. When he opened his eyes and scowled at her she grinned widely and stuck her tongue out at him.

"Remind me again why I have not simply squashed you under my thumb?" Val asked.

She turned and wiggled her ass at him before quickly kissing his lower lip and flying back to Abigail and Sara. She hovered in front of Sara and Abby smiled. "You see? Even the pixie is not afraid of him."

Val scowled at Abby. She winked at him as Sara held her hand out hesitantly. After a moment, Violet landed on it and Sara lifted her to her face to study her more closely.

"Hello, Violet," she whispered.

Violet waved at her before leaning forward and sniffing curiously at Sara's face. She flew from her hand with a sudden whirring of wings and landed on her shoulder before touching the curly blonde hair. She pulled on a strand of her hair, straightening it out and then grinning delightedly when she released it and it sprang back into a tight curl. She clapped her hands with delight before suddenly diving into Sara's mass of blonde curls.

Sara gave a squeak of surprise before giggling. "It tickles."

Abby grinned. "You get used to it. Are you hungry, Sara?"

"Yes. They hardly feed us in the slave quarters.".

"Then let's give you something to eat. You are much too

thin." Abigail brought her the tray of food and Sara eyed it hungrily.

"Eat, honey. There's plenty." Abigail urged.

As Sara began to eat, Abby smiled happily at Val. He shook his head in mock disappointment and closed his eyes again.

"WELL, SHE'S A PRETTY LITTLE THING." FAREN EXAMINED the sleeping Sara closely. "If you don't want her, Val, I'll take her."

"She's a human being, Faren," Abigail said. "Not some dog that you can just pass from one owner to another."

"All right, all right." Faren stepped away from the bed. "I was just offering."

He gave Val a scrutinizing look. "How are you feeling?"

"Perfectly fine."

"You look better."

"Obviously," Abigail snorted.

"No, I meant he looks better than he did even before the beatin," Faren replied. "Thirteen months without human blood is too long for any vampire."

"Thirteen months?" Abby whispered. She stared at Val and he was dismayed to feel a blush rising in his cheeks.

"I know, right? He's an idiot," Faren said cheerfully. "I'm surprised he didn't keel over. Animal blood only gives you so much energy."

He walked toward the door of the bedroom. "Are you coming to the common room?"

Val shook his head. "Not tonight. Abby needs more rest, and after what they did to me last night I'm not keen on joining them."

"I don't blame you."

"You need to be careful, Faren," Val suddenly said. "It would be wise for you to not join Darius tonight either."

"Yes, you're probably right." Faren sighed. "I will have them send the chubby one to my room."

"Her name is Sienna." Abigail scowled at him. "Make sure you are kind to her."

"I always am." Faren winked at her before leaving the room.

Abby touched Sara's hair. She didn't move, and Abby smiled faintly when she realized that Violet was sleeping in the girl's hair.

"You cannot keep her, Abigail," Val said in a low voice.

Abby sighed before joining him by the fire. She sat in his lap and rested her head against his shoulder.

"She's completely alone, Val. Did you really want me to leave her to Tavien? She's a sweetheart and you know it."

"That isn't the point. She's an added complication that we do not need."

"Tavien would have beaten and raped her. You can't honestly expect that I would be okay with that?"

"I'm not either but you cannot take in every stray waif that catches your attention."

She laughed. "She was offered to you as a gift. There was nothing wrong with accepting it. In fact, it probably helps lessen Darius' suspicion of you."

Val cupped her head and tugged until she looked up at him. "I am not sure that even now he believes I am Joven."

"I know. Tomorrow morning, I will kill the shifters guarding the slave quarters and Wesley, Evan and I will kill Darius and the others."

He studied her pale face and the dark circles under her eyes before shaking his head. "It's not a good idea, Abigail.

You're still tired and weak because of the blood I took from you. You will not be able to defeat the shifters in your current state."

"I'm fine," she said stubbornly.

"You are not." He scowled at her. "Wait one more day. Tomorrow night there is another round of games. The vampires will be tired from their night of revelry and will sleep more deeply during the day. It is better to do it then."

"Val, I -"

"Promise me, little dove. Wait one more day."

She didn't want to admit it, but Val was right. She *was* tired and feeling weak. She bent her head and kissed him. "I promise."

"Good." He glanced at the sleeping Sara. "You should join her in the bed."

"I will in a bit." She stroked his cheek until he looked at her. "Was it really thirteen months, Val?"

He looked away and she frowned and forced his gaze back to hers. "Tell me."

"Yes. I spent the first few months searching desperately for you and then, when I believed you to be dead, I couldn't stomach the thought of drinking another's blood. It is you I want, Abby. Only you."

He said the last in a soft mutter and she kissed his warm mouth. "I want you too, my love."

She deepened the kiss, sliding her tongue into his mouth and flicking it gently against his. He groaned and his hands tightened around her hips as she ducked her head and licked his throat.

"Little dove, we cannot. You need your rest," he said raggedly as she reached between them and stroked his cock through his pants.

"I need you," she whispered. The need for him, the almost

overwhelming urge for him to bite her, had returned but it didn't bother her. She had loved him before allowing him to feed from her again, and she felt only a warm rightness.

"The girl – your new pet – is right there," he gritted out.

She grinned. "I never took you to be a prude, Val. I sucked your cock in a room full of vampires and you fucked me in a hallway where anyone could have watched."

"That was different," he protested.

"It isn't. Besides, I don't think she'll wake up. She's exhausted. We'll just have to be very quiet." Abby unbuttoned his pants and slid her hand in to wrap around his thick shaft.

"I need you. Will you deny me?" She whispered into his ear.

"No," he groaned, "I will not."

"Good." She gave him a cat-like smile of satisfaction before tugging his cock free of his pants. He took another look at Sara. She was still sleeping soundly on the bed and he slid his hand under Abigail's skirt.

He rubbed her clit and she moaned before unhooking her bikini top. He sucked her nipple into his mouth greedily, rubbing at it with his tongue as his other hand traced the scarring on her back.

"You're so beautiful," he whispered.

"Thank you." She smiled sweetly at him before rubbing her thumb over the tip of his cock. "You're beautiful too."

He slid two fingers into her, probing deeply as she rubbed her pelvis against him. "Fuck me, Val. Please."

"Whatever you want, little dove," he breathed.

He lifted her and she guided his cock into her wet warmth. As she sank down onto him he groaned loudly. She clapped her hand over his mouth.

"Hush, my love. Do not wake her." She glanced over her

shoulder at the bed as he cupped her breasts and pulled on her nipples.

Her back arched and she bounced up and down on his cock as he tried to stop his loud groans. He reached between them and thumbed her clit. Her body stiffened and then she was clenching around his cock, her hands digging into his shoulders as she stifled her cries of pleasure.

"Bite me, Val," she pleaded in a soft voice. "Bite me!"

"I cannot," he groaned. "Not this time."

She made a soft sound of displeasure but didn't ask again. Panting harshly, he plunged in and out of her until, his cock swelling and his balls tightening, he came with a hoarse moan. He stared at her neck hungrily as his fangs lengthened, but he controlled the urge to bite her with a fierce determination. She could not afford to lose more blood. She shuddered above him and collapsed against his chest.

He stroked her back, the familiar rage rising up in him at the feel of the scars. If he could, he would find this woman - this foster mother - and tear her apart for what she had done to his dove.

She burrowed closer to him as he softened inside of her and gave a sigh of contentment. Her body was warm and lax against him, and he hugged her closely before doing up her bikini top and lifting her off of him.

She swayed on her feet and made a muttered sound of disapproval. He kissed her as he buttoned his pants. "Time for bed, little dove."

"Hmm…"

He carried her to the bed and tucked her in beside the blonde woman. She slid her hand under her pillow and sighed again as he sat down next to her. He stroked her hair as he studied her face.

She loved him. His heart sped up and he felt another unfamiliar rush of happiness. She loved him.

And you love her.

His hand froze against her soft hair for a moment before he rested his hand on her hip. He did love her. God help them both, but he did.

He leaned down and put his mouth to her ear. "Little dove?"

She didn't stir and he rested his face against her hair for a moment before whispering, "I love you."

CHAPTER 16

"Did he take the slave?" Darius, sitting apart from the others in the common room, arched his brow at Tavien.

"He did, my lord, but only because his current pet asked him to take her." Tavien sat down beside him and the two of them watched the other vampires in the room.

"Do you still doubt that he is Joven?" Darius asked.

Tavien hesitated and Darius waved his hand at him irritably. "Speak your mind, Tavien."

"I do, my lord."

"We tortured him quite badly last night and he did not break," Darius mused.

"True," Tavien replied. "But that proves only that he can withstand pain."

"I do not believe he is Joven," Darius said. "The real question is – why is he here if he is not? And who is his slave? She is not like any human female I've seen before."

"She is unique," Tavien agreed.

"I have never seen a woman fight so well with a sword before. Have you?"

"No."

"She would make an excellent addition to the games," Darius said. "How many vampires are in the estate right now, Tavien?"

"Not many, my lord. Most of them are out hunting." Tavien gave him an eager look. "Do you mean to kill the imposter?"

"I do. And I will take his slave as my own. She will fight in the games and warm my bed."

"I will gather what men we have and -"

Darius held up his hand. "Wait, Tavien. Are you not the least bit curious as to who he really is and why he is here?"

Tavien shrugged. "Not really."

Darius rolled his eyes. "That is why I am ruler and you are not, Tavien."

Tavien flushed, a grimace crossing his face as Darius stared at him. "I want to know why he is here. I want to know why he is so fond of the slave girl and why he only fed from her when he was dying. I have seen vampires who have not been feeding regularly, and this Joven bore all the markings of being hungry."

He gazed into the fire. "I'll admit I am impressed at how well he bore his punishment last night. If that's how he is when he is hungry and weak, can you imagine his power now that he has fed?"

"That's exactly why we should be killing him now, my lord. Before he becomes even more dangerous."

"It is a pity we'll have to kill him. A vampire like him would do well in my household. Perhaps if we used the slave as a bargaining chip…"

He sat silently for a moment before shaking his head. "No. He is not a vampire who will be told what to do. We'll have to kill him."

Tavien breathed a sigh of relief. "I will take care of it tonight, my lord."

Darius grunted in annoyance. "Hold off, Tavien. We will kill him but first I want to know who he is."

"My lord, there is no way of -"

"He came with two other slaves, did he not?" Darius asked.

"Yes. They are in the slave quarters." Tavien's eyes gleamed as he stared at Darius.

"Bring one of them to me."

"Which one, my lord?"

"The bigger of the two."

"WHAT IS YOUR NAME?" DARIUS STARED AT THE DARK-skinned man standing before him. He was tall and broad, and his bare skull gleamed in the torch light.

"Wesley," the man grunted.

"Do you enjoy being Lord Joven's slave?"

"Where is the Lord Joven?" Wesley asked.

Darius gave him an admiring look. The human was in a room with powerful vampires, but he could smell no fear radiating from him. "You are brave for a human."

Wesley didn't reply, and Darius leaned back in his chair and crossed his legs. "Tell me who he really is."

"Who?"

"The man pretending to be Lord Joven. I want to know his real name."

"He is the Lord Joven." Wesley gave him a confused look.

Darius chuckled. "I know he is not. Now tell me his real name or suffer the consequences."

"His name is Joven."

Darius sighed irritably and waved his hand at Tavien. Tavien was standing on Wesley's right side. Without a word, he grabbed the big man's forearm and twisted it sharply to the right. There was a loud crack and Wesley screamed as his skin split open and white bone protruded.

Blood poured out of his arm and both Darius and Tavien licked their lips as Wesley, his face turning grey, clutched at his broken arm.

"Tell me his name," Darius demanded.

"His name is Joven."

With a soft hiss, Darius moved. He was nothing but a blur and Wesley cried out when Darius grabbed him by the neck and dragged him forward. He tried to struggle back but the vampire was incredibly strong, and he screamed hoarsely as Darius sunk his fangs deep into his neck. He drank until Wesley fell to his knees. His head dropped forward, and he panted harshly as his eyes closed.

Darius crouched before him and tapped him on the fore-head. "His real name. Give it to me now."

"Joven."

"You are going to die. Do you hear me? I have drank you nearly dry and you have, maybe, minutes left in your stupid, insignificant life. You will tell me what I want to know."

With great effort, Wesley lifted his head. "I will die before I tell you anything."

Darius grinned. "You will tell me everything."

He brought his own wrist to his mouth and with a flick of his fangs, sliced the skin open. As dark blood poured down his pale skin, he grinned again at Wesley. "You will make an excellent vampire, my dark-skinned friend."

Wesley's eyes widened and with one last burst of energy, staggered to his feet. He lurched toward the door and Tavien, laughing under his breath, tripped him. He fell to the floor with a harsh thud and rolled onto his back.

He clamped his mouth shut as Darius leaned over him and held his bleeding wrist over his mouth. Blood poured onto Wesley's face and closed mouth and, with a sigh of annoyance, Darius glanced at Tavien. "Open his mouth."

"Yes, my lord."

He kneeled on Wesley's chest and forced his mouth open. Wesley made a gurgling scream as the blood poured into his mouth and tried desperately to spit it out. Darius laughed and held his wrist closer to his mouth until the blood was flowing thick and heavy into Wesley's mouth.

Wesley went rigid, his eyes closing and his hands clenching into fists, before his back arched and he bucked Tavien off of him. His eyes popped open. Their dark brown colour was slowly fading to the golden colour of honey. Darius grinned when he clamped his mouth around his wrist and drank eagerly.

"STAY CLOSE TO ME," VAL MURMURED AS THEY FOLLOWED Darius and Tavien to the arena. "Something doesn't feel right."

Abigail nodded as Sara gripped her hand tightly. Val was right. Darius and Tavien were acting no differently but she couldn't ignore the warning tingle at the base of her spine. Something was very wrong.

She gave Sara a reassuring smile that turned into a grimace when she saw Violet's face peek out of the woman's blonde girls.

"What is she doing here?" She muttered to Sara.

"She didn't want to be left in the room," Sara whispered.

"Keep her hidden," Abigail warned.

Sara nodded, cringing a little when they entered the arena and she caught a glimpse of the vampires sitting in the stands. "Abby?"

"It'll be fine." Abigail squeezed her hand again as Val sat down. She sat on the pillow at his feet, urging Sara to sit beside her.

There was a loud crack of thunder, and lightning flashed across the sky. The wind was picking up and Sara huddled against her as the first few drops of cold rain fell from the sky.

Darius glanced at the sky. "We are in for quite a storm tonight. Don't you agree, Lord Joven?"

"Yes." Val nodded to Faren when he joined them. Sienna trailed after him and she sat at his feet as he stroked her hair.

"Where is Jaxen?" Val asked abruptly.

"There was a matter I've asked him to attend to," Darius replied.

Val glanced at Abby. She was giving him an anxious look and he squeezed her shoulder.

Darius stood and waited patiently for the crowd of vampires to quiet. "My friends, welcome! Tonight, we have something very special in mind and I believe you'll be immensely entertained by it."

The crowd cheered loudly. Darius raised his hands and motioned for them to quiet. "Let us begin!"

The thick wooden doors to the arena opened and Ursula stepped into the arena. She stared silently at the crowd as they roared their approval. Abigail waited tensely to see who her opponent would be. She did not believe it would be Maria, but she couldn't relax until she knew for sure.

The minutes passed and when a second fighter did not

join Ursula, the crowd murmured impatiently. Darius, still standing, grinned as Tavien stood.

"Are you ready for her opponent?" Darius shouted.

The crowd screamed yes. Abby, scanning the arena anxiously, felt Val's hand on her shoulder tighten. She glanced up at him, her gaze widening when she realized Tavien was holding his sword to Val's chest.

Darius grinned at her and held out his hand. "Come, my pet. The crowd waits for you."

"No!" Val snarled. He started to stand and hissed when Tavien pressed his sword into his chest and blood bloomed on his shirt.

"Be still, Lord Joven. Unless you want to die tonight?" Darius said. He turned to Abigail. "You will fight the large bitch or watch your master die."

"Abigail, do not -"

She ignored Val and stood up. "Don't kill him. I will do what you ask."

"Excellent." Darius pointed to the arena. "Go on, then. Show us what you can do."

Her heart thudding and adrenaline singing in her veins, Abby bent and quickly kissed Val on the mouth. "I love you."

She turned and leaped nimbly over the stone wall in front of them. She landed in the dirt with a soft thud and walked to the center of the arena. Ursula scowled at her.

"You are the one who killed my sister."

"She gave me no choice," Abigail replied.

"I'm going to enjoy hurting you. You will suffer more than any human has suffered in this arena."

Abby stared silently at her as two vampires appeared and handed them each a sword. She breathed a sigh of relief at the weapon choice and gripped it tightly as she glanced back at Val. Tavien still held his sword to his chest and he was staring at her with a look of fear on his face. She gave him a reassuring smile as the vampires disappeared and left her alone with Ursula.

With a sudden shriek of rage, Ursula charged at her. She swung her sword and Abigail blocked it, nearly collapsing under the weight of the larger woman's swing. She backed away as Ursula grinned at her.

"You're such a puny, weak human. I don't know how you bested my sister."

"Your sister was slow and clumsy," Abby taunted. She had seen the woman fight before and she wanted her to be angry. Anger had a way of making a person careless, making them lose their concentration. She smiled with satisfaction when Ursula howled again and attacked.

The vampires were cheering and screaming but Abigail paid no attention to them. She swung and parried and thrust her sword as the two women moved around the arena. Their blades clashed repeatedly. Ursula gave an inarticulate bellow of rage and pain when Abby's blade slipped past hers and sliced across her midsection.

She clapped her hand over her stomach and stared at the blood slipping through her fingers before raising her gaze to Abby. "You bitch! I'll kill you. I swear it!"

"You'll be seeing your sister soon," Abby said. "Tell her I said hello, would you?"

Ursula hesitated. Abby attacked her, swinging her sword in a short and powerful arc. Ursula raised her sword and blocked it before swinging her fist at Abby. Abigail ducked and charged forward. She grabbed Ursula's wrist, twisting brutally until the woman screamed and the sword dropped from her numb fingers, and then thrust her sword into Ursula's stomach.

The larger woman made a soft grunt of disbelief and

stared at the sword protruding from her belly. She blinked rapidly and stared at Abby as blood began to drizzle from her mouth. There was another loud crack of thunder and the skies opened. Cold rain fell in sheets, drenching both her and Ursula and washing away the blood from her sword when she pulled it free from the woman's flesh.

Ursula dropped to her knees and reached toward Abby with one groping hand. The anger had left her face, leaving only a weary look of fear and resignation. Abby reached out and took her hand. She was suddenly horrified by what she had done, and she dropped her sword and crouched in front of Ursula.

"I'm sorry," she whispered as the woman stared at her with dark eyes.

"See my sister…soon," Ursula gasped as more blood trickled from her mouth. She collapsed onto her back.

Abby wiped the rainwater from the woman's face. "Yes, you will see her soon."

"Good," Ursula wheezed. "Tired."

"I know," Abby whispered. "Close your eyes, Ursula."

The big woman nodded and let her eyelids shut. Her breathing was growing shallow and Abby continued to stroke her face until she took one final shuddering breath and died.

Feeling tired and sick to her stomach, Abby picked up her sword and stood. She turned to face Darius.

"Are you happy, Lord Darius?" She shouted above the wind and the thunder. "Was it a good enough show for you?"

He laughed and fear flooded through her when three of his men appeared beside Val and Faren. They urged them to their feet and prodded them with their swords to move into the arena.

"Send their slaves with them," Darius demanded. "I do not need them either."

Sara and Sienna were pushed into place behind them and the four of them were herded quickly into the middle of the arena. Val put his arm around Abby as Darius and Tavien stood in front of them.

Darius stared at the arena of vampires as the wind whipped his long, wet hair around his face.

"My friends," he shouted. "This vampire says he is the Lord Joven. I welcomed him into my home, offered him a soft bed, warm women, and a chance to take part in the games. Was that not generous of me?"

The vampires nodded, a few of them shouting out 'yes', as Darius turned to Val. "I know who you really are, Valkyn, son of Maridus."

Val's arm tightened around Abigail's waist as Faren sighed. "Well, fuck. We're all dead."

"What I did not understand was what happened to the real Joven and why you took his place," Darius said. The wind was rising, and the thunder was almost continuous now. Lightning flashed across the sky, illuminating the arena in stark relief.

"However, that mystery was solved last night." Darius turned to the vampires standing guard at the wooden doors. "Bring them out."

The doors opened and Jaxen, Michael, Neil, Maria and Evan entered the arena. Fear trickled through Abby as they joined her and the others.

"Evan, where is Wesley?" She asked.

"I don't know," he said. "They took him last night and I have not seen him since."

"Are you looking for your dark-skinned friend?" Darius asked. "Shall I call him?"

Without waiting for their reply, he shouted Wesley's

name. Abby and Evan gave matching groans of dismay when Wesley strode into the arena.

"Oh Wesley," Abby whispered.

Wesley grinned at her and Evan cursed violently at the sight of his long fangs. "Hello, Abigail."

"Your friend has been quite helpful to us," Darius said. "Once we turned him, he told us everything we needed to know about your pathetic little rescue attempt."

He turned and studied Michael intently. "Is this man really worth it? I know for sure that these two are not." He glanced dismissively at Neil and Maria.

When they didn't reply, Darius sighed and glanced at Tavien. "Humans, they are ridiculous, are they not?"

"Yes, my lord."

"I can understand why they would want to rescue their friends, they are too tender-hearted for their own good, but why on earth would vampires align themselves with the humans?"

He gave Jaxen a look of false sorrow. "Jaxen, my old friend, I am most disappointed in you."

"You are not my friend," Jaxen said.

"That hurts me. You have spent many months living in my home, taking your fill of my slaves, and this is how you repay me?"

Darius stepped closer and Abigail raised the sword she still held as Val pulled his free from his belt. Darius rolled his eyes. "Please, do you believe that either of you have a chance against us?"

"You do not have that many men," Val said.

Darius chuckled with amusement. "I suppose that is true, but you forget who our audience is."

He stared at the crowd. "This vampire – this imposter –

has made an alliance with the humans. What do you think of that? Does he deserve our mercy?"

The crowd screamed angrily, and a few of the vampires in the lower stands actually leaped over the stone wall and began to close in around them. Darius stopped them with a wave of his hand. "All in good time, my friends."

"Jaxen, come to me," he encouraged.

"Don't, Jaxen!" Abigail said sharply.

"He has no choice," Darius replied.

"Jaxen," Abby whispered.

"It will be all right." He smiled at her and moved jerkily to Darius. He stood in front of the larger man, his fine white hair sticking to his head as the rain poured down, and folded his arms behind his back.

"Why would you betray me, Jaxen?" Darius asked with genuine puzzlement.

"The humans are not ours to control, Darius. All creatures deserve freedom, deserve the right to live their life without being -"

"Boring," Darius said.

His hands snaked out and Sienna and Sara both screamed shrilly when he ripped Jaxen's head from his body. The old man's body crumpled to the ground as blood poured from the stump of his neck.

"I never really liked him anyway." Darius grinned at Tavien before dropping Jaxen's head. His body and head exploded, and the blood and ash was immediately washed away by the hard rain.

"You son of a bitch!" Abby cried. She started forward but Val's arm snapped around her waist and pulled her back.

"Let go of me!" She shouted.

"Be still!" Val hissed into her ear. She slumped against

him as Wesley stepped forward. He reached out, ignoring Val's growl, and stroked Abby's cheek.

"I was wrong to fear it, Abigail." His eyes were a golden brown now and they glowed with a hellish light. "It is," he paused, "beautiful. This is a gift."

Evan, the freckles standing out on his face in pale relief, shoved Wesley away from Abby and glared at the larger man. "Don't touch her, you fucking leech!"

With a snarl of rage, Wesley yanked Evan into his embrace and yanked his head back.

"Wesley! Don't -"

He lowered his head and sunk his fangs into Evan's neck. Darius laughed and clapped his hands delightedly as the big man tore Evan's throat open and lapped at the blood like a dog.

Abby stared in horror at Wesley. "What have you done?"

Wesley dropped Evan's body and licked the blood from his lips. There was more blood smeared across his cheeks and chin and he wiped at it with his hand before licking the blood from his palm. "It is a gift, Abigail."

"It is," Darius agreed. "Unfortunately, it is not one you will ever know. We're not going to turn you, my pet. We're going to keep you as human and use you in the games. First, we'll kill your friends," he glanced at Michael, "except for your beloved Michael, of course, he's too valuable to simply kill. And then we'll chain your master and let him slowly starve as he watches me feed from you."

"You're going to die tonight," Val said.

Darius laughed again. "My friend, there are so few of you and so many of us – you don't stand a chance and you know it."

He smiled at Abigail. "Take Wesley's hand, my pet, and I

will end your friends' lives quickly and painlessly. Disobey me and you will watch them suffer."

Abigail glanced at Val and his eyes widened in horror. "No! Do not, little dove! Do you hear me?"

"Shh, my love. It will be all right." She kissed him on the mouth. "Do not fight, Val. They will tear you apart."

"Listen to your slave, Valkyn," Darius advised. "I would prefer to watch you starve to death, but I won't hesitate to take your head if you insist on," he paused and laughed, "making a scene."

"Abigail," Val muttered.

"Trust me, my love," she breathed into his ear.

Holding her sword loosely in her left hand, she took a few hesitant steps forward. Wesley smiled and held out his hand. She took it, shuddering a little at his touch. His hand tightened around hers and his fangs lengthened.

"Just one taste, Abby," he whispered.

He yanked her forward. Abby began to cry as his eyes widened and he gave her a blank look of surprise.

"I'm so sorry, Wesley," she whispered.

His gaze dropped to his chest. Abby had skewered him through the heart, and he gave her another puzzled look before he burst apart in a shower of ash and blood. Abby wiped the hot blood from her face and backed away toward Val and the others. She was covered in ash and blood and she lifted her face to the sky and let the rain wash it clean.

"You stupid little bitch!" Darius snarled. "Your friends will die cursing your name!"

He motioned for the other vampires. As they began to close in around them, Abigail and the others formed a tight circle.

"What the fuck do we do now?" Faren shouted as thunder, this one so close it shook the ground beneath their feet, boomed above them.

"We fight," Michael said.

"Right, of course." Faren rolled his eyes before pulling the dagger from his belt. "Here, take this. You're probably better with it than I am."

Michael took it as a flash of lightning struck the ground only a few feet away from them.

"Bring them to me, now!" Darius suddenly shouted.

Before the vampires could attack, there was another bolt of lightning and a few of the vampires in the stands screamed as it struck the stands and sent vampires scattering.

The wind became a screaming, shrieking moan and everyone glanced around uneasily when the air began to crackle. The hair on Abigail's arms was standing on end and there was a strange hum of electricity.

"What is happening?" Darius turned to Tavien. "What is -"

He cried out when there was a loud snap of electricity and the arena was lit up with a brilliant, golden light.

"Oh my God," Abby breathed.

A small yellow orb was hovering behind them. As they watched, it grew steadily larger. It hummed and crackled with power and Sienna gave a shout of fear when she was pulled off her feet. She was being dragged toward the glowing orb and Neil reached out and snagged her arm. He yanked her to her feet and held her against his body as Abby grabbed Val's arm frantically.

"Val! It is our only chance!" She screamed at him.

He shook his head. "No, we cannot! We don't know where it will go!"

"Anywhere is better than here!" Neil shouted. He held Sienna's hand in his left and grabbed Maria's in his right.

Before they could stop him, he dragged them forward. They were caught in the light of the orb and there were screams of shocks from the vampires in the arena when they were sucked forward and disappeared.

"Michael! Take Sara and go!" Abby shouted.

Violet, her wings fluttering violently in the wind, zipped out from Sara's hair and dived into Abby's. She could feel the pixie clinging tightly to her scalp as she grabbed Michael's arm and shook him.

"Go, Michael!"

She pushed Sara forward, the woman gave a shriek of fear and tried to back away, but Michael took her hand and with one last grim look at Abby, pulled her into the orb.

"Wha- what is going on?" Darius asked in a soft little mutter. The sight of the orb and the humans disappearing into it had seemed to completely disarm him and he backed away as the light washed over him.

"Tavien? What dark magic is this?" He whined.

There was no reply and he looked around in surprise. Tavien had fled to the far end of the arena. Darius turned back to the orb and stared into its depths.

"Faren, move!" Val suddenly roared.

Faren shook his head. "No way, count me out. I'm not going anywhere near that thing."

He shouted in surprise when Val gave him a hard shove toward the orb. He was bathed in the orb's light and he scrabbled madly for a moment before the orb lifted him off his feet and sucked him into its relentless glowing light. He disappeared, and Abby took Val's hand.

"Let's go!" She shouted.

He cupped her face and pressed his mouth against her ear. "I love you, little dove."

He kissed her hard and shoved her toward the orb before turning and moving in a blur of speed to Darius.

He swung his sword and a small smile of satisfaction crossed his face when Darius' head slid from his body and fell into the wet dirt. As the vampire's body exploded, Abigail screamed his name. She had fallen on her stomach but was rising into the air as she was dragged into the orb. She stretched her arms out and screamed his name again as her hands reached for him.

He dropped his sword and dove for Abigail and the light, his hands stretching for hers. As her fingers closed around his wrists and gripped tightly, he closed his eyes and felt his body being flung forward. There was a stomach-dropping sensation of falling and a brief moment of pain before everything went black.

———

"VAL? VAL, OPEN YOUR EYES." HER SOFT VOICE DRAGGED him from the dark and he opened his eyes and blinked blearily at her.

She was lying on top of him, her face only inches from his. He kissed her hard. She returned his kiss, her hands stroking his hair and face before she pulled back.

"I love you," he said hoarsely. "I love you."

"I love you too," she said before kissing him again.

"I hate to interrupt this beautiful moment," Faren's voice drawled above them, "but maybe one of you could tell me what the fuck just happened."

They staggered to their feet and a look of fear crossed Abigail's face as she reached into her hair. "Violet! Violet, where are you!"

The pixie appeared in front of her, hovering in the air and grinning widely at her.

Abby breathed a sigh of relief. "Thank God. Don't do that to me, little one."

Violet landed on Val's shoulder and kissed his cheek before clinging to his dark hair.

"What the fuck just happened?" Faren suddenly shouted. "Where the fuck are we?"

Abigail looked around. They were in the middle of a forest and although it was dark, the moon was large and bright and provided enough light for her to see. "We're on another world, Faren."

"Oh great." Faren raked his hand through his wet hair. "That's just fucking great. How the hell do we get back?"

"We don't," Abby said.

She walked toward Maria and Neil and squeezed their hands. Sienna was clinging to Neil's waist, and he kept one arm firmly around her. "Are you two all right?"

"Yes." Maria shivered delicately. "Freezing but glad to be alive."

"We'll build a fire," Abby said. "It will be okay, Maria."

She turned toward Michael and Sara. "Are either of you -"

She stuttered to a stop. Michael was sitting under a tree, his back resting against its rough bark, and staring at his hands.

"Michael? Where is Sara?" Abby glanced around wildly. "Sara! Sara, answer me!"

"She let go of my hand," Michael said hoarsely. "We were being sucked into the orb and she let go of my hand. I tried to grab her again, I swear it, but she wasn't there."

"Oh no," Abby moaned. She gave Val a frantic look. "We

have to find her! She can't be far. We need to start searching for her and -"

"We'll find her, little dove," Val said. "I promise you. But we need to -"

He suddenly stiffened and stared into the dark trees around them. "Someone is coming."

The others scrambled to join them, and they stared in the direction that Val was looking in.

"Who is it?" Abby whispered as Violet disappeared into Val's hair.

Val shook his head. "I don't know. I can't see them yet. I can hear them though and they -"

There was a low growling behind them, and the group swung around. Abby's eyes widened. A wolf, the biggest one she'd ever seen, was standing only ten feet away. His eyes were a bright, glowing green, and his grey fur was rippling in the breeze.

There was more soft growling as two other wolves appeared out of the darkness.

"Does anyone have a weapon?" Abby whispered. She had lost her sword as the orb had sucked her in and she could see the sheath around Val's waist hanging empty.

Michael gave a soft grunt and held up the dagger that Faren had given him. "I have this."

"We don't need weapons," Maria said. "We have Val."

Val hissed at the wolves, and they chuffed in surprise when they saw the fangs protruding from his mouth.

"Val, wait." Abby grabbed his arm. "Just wait and -"

The largest wolf suddenly rippled violently. They watched as the fur receded and the wolf became a man. He was a giant of a man and he studied them quietly as the other two wolves shifted and joined him.

"Shifters," Faren breathed. "Perhaps we are still on our world, after all."

One of the men frowned and glanced up at the larger man. "What manner of creature has teeth like that, Kane? And why do they smell so," he wrinkled his nose, "dreadful."

"I do not know, Hanif," the man named Kane replied.

Faren sighed loudly. "Fuck. Not our world. Stupid fucking ball of light sending us who the fuck knows where."

Kane stiffened and frowned at him. "What did you say, creature?"

"Creature? I have a name," Faren said.

Kane growled loudly and Faren hissed at him as Abby held her hands up hurriedly.

"Okay, um, before we get off on the wrong foot, let's just everyone take a deep breath. My name's Abby and these are my friends, and we're not from around here. So, we're just going to head on out and um, it was really great to meet you. Take care, okay?"

Kane growled again and took a step toward her. Val pushed Abby behind him and bared his fangs at the large, naked man. "Take one more step toward her and I'll have your head."

"I would like to see you try," Kane said. "I don't know what you are, but you do not frighten me."

Val glared at him. "You would be wise to be frightened of me, shifter."

"Val, stop!" Abigail squeezed his arm and gave Kane a friendly smile. "We're friendly, honestly. And if you would just step aside, we'll be on our way."

"You are on my lands," Kane said. "Tell me, and do not lie about this, if what the creature said about the ball of light is true."

Abigail hesitated and then nodded. "Yes, it's true."

The smallest of the three men squeezed Kane's arm before inhaling deeply in Abigail's direction. "She smells like Reese."

"Yes, Theran. I am aware of that," Kane said.

He studied them for a moment before coming to a quick decision. "You will come with us."

"I don't think so," Val said.

"You have no choice," Kane said.

"There are only three of you and six of us," Val replied. "You do not stand a chance."

Kane surprised them by laughing loudly. "You are a brave one. Foolish, but brave."

He lifted his head and barked roughly. Abby gripped Val's arm when a chorus of barking responded and the trees around them were lit with dozens of glowing eyes.

Sienna gave a soft whimper of fear and Neil hugged her close. "Do not worry." He gave her an encouraging smile, but his face was pale as more eyes appeared in the darkness.

"Our pack is large," Kane said with a hint of pride in his voice. "You are returning to our home and you will neither fight nor try to escape. Do you understand?"

Val opened his mouth to argue and Abigail gripped his arm and gave him a warning look before smiling at Kane. "Of course. Thank you for the hospitality."

Kane grunted in reply and shifted to his wolf form before turning and loping into the trees. The other wolves surrounded them in a tight circle and Maria cleared her throat. "What do we do now?"

"We go with them," Abigail replied. "He's right - we don't have much choice."

She took Val's hand and gave him a faint smile as they followed Kane and the others through the trees. "Everything will work out. We will find Sara, and you and I will make a new life together on this world. I love you, Val."

He raised her hand to his mouth and pressed a soft kiss to her knuckles. "I love you too, little dove."

END

Keep reading for an excerpt to Book Three, The Shifteer's Mate.

THE SHIFTER'S MATE EXCERPT

(OTHER WORLD SERIES BOOK 3)

All things considered, it hadn't been the worse three months of Reese Warren's life. That top honour still went to the months following her parents' deaths. But the last three months certainly were the weirdest.

As she paced restlessly back and forth in the room she had begun to think of as the 'waiting room', she wished for the hundredth time that she had never gone outside to investigate the round ball of light hovering in the back yard.

She almost hadn't. She had almost chalked it up to some weird surge of electricity from the massive thunder and lightning storm and gone to bed, but in the end her natural curiosity couldn't be contained.

She snorted bitterly. Her mother had always told her that curiosity killed the cat and although it hadn't killed her, it hadn't prepared her to be sucked into some alternate universe like a woman in a bad science fiction movie.

Not an alternate universe, Reese. An alternate world. God, pay attention, would you?

She could almost hear Louisa's disapproving tone in her head. She sighed and sank to the floor beside the barred window. She missed the old woman, missed her more than she would admit. She had been the only link to her world, to *her* earth. With her gone, she was terribly lonely.

It's your own fault, she scolded herself fiercely. *Louisa tried to warn you to keep your mouth shut about your earth, but you didn't listen, did you? You just had to try and convince them that electricity and cars, and airplanes and stores that served nothing but coffee, existed. Tried to convince them that a giant globe of light had sucked you in and threw you down into this strange world.*

The men who had captured her only hours after she had walked out of the woods, dirty and bruised, had laughed and called her "barto". She had found out later that barto was the word for crazy in this world.

Perhaps because she was still numb from the deaths of her parents, perhaps because she half-believed she was in some strange never-ending dream, she hadn't really freaked out when the men had chained her and taken her to a large, gated complex. She was left in a room full of other women. They were nice enough to her at first, at least until she started babbling about her own world, and after that they avoided her.

Only Louisa had gone near her and that was only because she was from the same world as Reese. She had taken Reese's arm in a firm grip and dragged her away as Reese was trying, very patiently she thought, to explain to a young woman named Rhea about cell phones and the internet.

It took Reese a few days to understand exactly what Louisa explained to her. Even now, three months later, she wasn't sure she still entirely believed that there was no way back home for her ever again.

She sighed and stared out the window. Louisa was taken to auction two weeks ago, and Reese missed her more than she thought possible. She hoped the old woman was okay, hoped that someone kind had bought her and was treating her well. She sighed again. She would never see Louisa again and now, it was her turn to go to auction.

The door to the room opened and Reese watched with a numb disinterest as the man she secretly called the "warden" walked through. He was followed by three of the biggest men she had ever seen in her life. All three of them had dark hair and dark eyes and they were all pulling and tugging on their clothing with obvious discomfort.

Malana was standing near her, her eyes wide and her mouth a quivering "o", as she stared at the three men. Reese tugged on the young woman's arm.

"What's going on? Are we not being taken to the auction room?"

Malana must have been truly desperate for comfort because she immediately wrapped her arms around Reese's waist and clung to her like a frightened child. "God help us."

"Help us from what?" Reese asked. "What's going on?"

"It's – it's a private sale," Malana whispered.

"Well, that has to be better than being paraded around like a cow in front of a roomful of men, doesn't it?" Reese replied.

Malana gave her a frightened look. "You don't understand. Those – those men are not men."

Reese glanced at them. They looked like men to her. Big men, but still just men. "What do you mean?"

"They're shifters, Reese," Malana whispered.

"What do you mean shifters?" Reese frowned at the smaller woman.

Malana gave her a look of frustration. "Shifters! They shift into animals."

Reese blinked in surprise. "What kind of animals?"

"If I had to guess, these ones are wolves or bears," Malana said. "They're so big."

She stared wide-eyed at the men. "We're dead if they choose us."

As the warden stood quietly and the three men talked amongst themselves, Reese rubbed Malana's trembling back. "Why would you say that?"

Malana swallowed hard. "Shifters rarely have anything to do with humans. Many of them hunt us like – like we're deer."

Reese felt a trickle of fear run down her spine. She took a deep breath and shook it off. "Why would they pay money for us just to hunt us down and kill us? Don't be silly."

Malana gave her a look of stark fear. "If they not buying us to hunt then they're buying us for sex. I would rather be hunted."

Before Reese could reply the warden moved to the middle of the room. "Line up, ladies!"

Reese and the other women - there were more than fifteen of them crowded into the small room - lined up obediently. The three men walked back and forth in front of them.

Malana squeezed Reese's hand painfully when their gazes landed on them and Reese winced. She tried to free her hand but Malana refused to let go until the men continued past them.

After a few moments, the men had a whispered conversation with the warden. He nodded and walked to the line of women. He pulled a few of them forward roughly. When he stopped in front of Reese and Malana, the young woman began to cry.

"Stop your blubbering, girl," he said. "They have no use for you."

He took Reese's shoulder and pulled her out of the line. "Stand there."

Reese and four other women stood silently as the warden herded the other women from the room. He shut the door and stared at the women.

"These men are going to look you over. Resist and you'll be beaten. Do you understand?"

The women nodded. A few of them were beginning to cry as two of the men stepped closer. Reese, her body trembling and her breathing shallow, straightened her back. If these men really were some kind of half-man, half-beast mutation, her job as a vet tech had taught her not to show fear around animals.

She watched with wide eyes as two of the men examined the women standing to her right. They had the women open their mouths so they could look at their teeth. The men held the women's faces, examining their eyes and probing at their ears like they really were cattle.

Her mouth dropped open and she took a step back when the men slipped their hands under the plain blue blouses that all of the women wore. When Reese first arrived, they had stripped her of all of her clothing except her underwear. She had been wearing the same blue blouse and brown skirt that the rest of the women wore since then. Although it was actually sort of freeing to not be wearing a bra, she wondered exactly what her heavy breasts would look like ten years from now. She was young enough that they were still perky but after years of no support, she guessed they'd be hanging around her goddamn knees.

She shook her head. What the hell was she doing? She was about to be touched and examined like a piece of meat and she was concerned about her breast perkiness? She snorted and forced her attention back to the other women. The men were squeezing their breasts before running their hands over their abdomens and then grabbing their asses through their long skirts. The smallest of the men even bent and lifted one woman's skirt, studying her thick calves and thighs with interest.

Reese realized that all four women were similar to her. Although she was the tallest and heaviest, all of the women had large breasts and wide hips. As the two men worked their way down the line, she felt the hot breath of the warden on the back of her neck.

"Behave yourself, woman," he snarled.

Reese tensed when she felt his hand stroke her back. "Keep that smart mouth of yours shut or the beatings you received before this will be nothing compared to the one you'll get," he warned.

Reese arched her back away from the despicable man's touch. She hated the warden, hated him with every fibre of her being. It was all she could do not to turn around and spit on him. Her temper had always gotten her in trouble, and it had been no different in this world. Even the frequent beatings she had received were not yet enough to curb her wayward tongue.

The smallest of the men stopped in front of her. He smiled at her in a friendly way and was about to reach for her when the third man stepped forward. Unlike his companions, he had not bothered to examine any of the women. He had stood back, staring at them with a bored expression on his face while the women were touched and examined.

"Move back, Theran." His voice was low and hoarse, as if he didn't use it much.

The man in front of her stepped away immediately and

Reese stared up at the man who took his place. She was just shy of six feet, but she still had to crane her neck to look at him. He was the biggest of the three men, and she judged his height to be somewhere around the seven-foot mark. His shoulders and chest were broad and thick with muscle. His lower body was clad in a pair of loose cotton pants, but she had no trouble seeing how thick and strong his thighs were.

Dark scruff covered his angular jaw, and she felt a strange twinge in her stomach when she stared at his full lips. She forced her gaze up to his and saw surprise in his dark eyes. The rest of the women had cowered and stared at the floor while they were being examined, but she would be damned if she stood meekly by while some strange man groped her.

He stared at her eyes and she wondered what he was thinking. They were her most striking feature. Technically they were considered blue, but in most light they looked very close to violet.

She stood still when his large hands cupped her face and his thumbs pressed at her mouth. She opened her mouth and did nothing when he examined her teeth before checking inside her ears and running his hands over her thick, dark hair.

His breath was warm on her face and she continued to stare at him as he ran his hands over her neck and shoulders. It wasn't until he reached for her breasts, that she jerked back and shoved him hard in the chest. He gave a grunt of surprise, his eyebrows drawing into a frown, but didn't stumble back. She might as well have tried shoving a large boulder.

She cried out when the warden's fist punched her hard in the middle of her back. Not expecting it, she pitched forward into the chest of the giant standing in front of her. She could feel his low growl vibrating in his chest, and his arms clamped around her hips when she started to struggle back.

"She's a wild one." The warden reached to cuff her across the head and Reese cringed. Before he could land the blow, the man holding her grabbed the warden's arm in one hard hand.

"Enough," he grunted.

The warden winced and nodded before stepping back and rubbing at his arm.

"Hold still, human," the giant rumbled.

Reese glared at him. It wasn't like she had much choice. His arm was still clamped around her hips and it was like a band of steel. Her back was throbbing where the warden had punched her, and she flinched when the man ran his hand down her back.

He frowned and moved his hand to her ass to squeeze it firmly. Reese hissed at him like an angry cat and slapped at his hand. He scowled and took her wrists in one large hand, holding them firmly.

"Hold still," he repeated.

His free hand reached for one full breast and Reese twisted violently in his grasp. "If you touch me there, I'll kill you."

He stared silently at her for a moment, his hand resting on her round abdomen, before dropping his hand to her hip. He rubbed it gently then slipped his hand under her shirt and stroked the bare skin of her side. She was dismayed to feel a tingle of lust go through her.

Shit, she thought frantically as a strange look came over his face. Big men had always been her weakness, perhaps because she was so tall herself, and this was the biggest man she'd ever met. It didn't help that he was actually kind of handsome with his dark eyes and full lips.

He leaned in and buried his face in her neck, inhaling deeply.

Goosebumps rose on her flesh and she whimpered when he suddenly licked her throat with his warm, wet tongue. She wasn't sure what was happening to her. Lust had roared to life within her and without realizing it, she leaned into his warm body.

This time when his hand reached for her breast, she made no attempt to struggle away. He cupped her bare breast, his thumb rubbing over her erect nipple, and she made another soft whimper of need.

She stumbled and nearly fell when he pulled away from her. She stared mutely at him, her pulse pounding and her blood roaring through her veins, as he snorted derisively and turned back to his companions.

"He'll like this one. She's easily aroused."

Reese's face flamed with embarrassment and she bent her head and stared at the floor. What the fuck had just happened?

The warden cleared his throat. "Are you sure you want this one? She's not obedient. I know your – your kind like your women submissive."

The man ignored him and stared at his companions. "Do you agree?"

The one named Theran shrugged. "We can't take just her. He wanted a choice, remember?"

The man snorted angrily. "So, we have to feed a bunch of humans because he could not be bothered to make the trip himself and pick out one."

The second man laughed. "They'll be useful in other ways. You know that as well as I do, Kane."

Kane sighed. "I never thought I would live to see the day we had humans in our pack."

The second man pulled at the collar of his shirt. "We cannot disobey our alpha's demands."

"I know that, Hanif. Do you believe me to be simple?" Kane growled.

"Of course not," Hanif said. He bowed his head in a show of submission to the bigger man.

"We will each pick one. He can choose from them. If he doesn't find any of them pleasing, he can come back and choose his own mate," Kane said with finality.

"We'll take her," he pointed to Reese, "and two more that my brothers will choose."

The warden nodded as Kane stepped forward and took Reese's wrist in one large hand. She pulled futilely, and he growled at her. "Enough or I will drag you from this room by your hair. Do you understand?"

She glared at him before following him towards the door.

ABOUT THE AUTHOR

Ramona Gray is a Canadian romance author. She currently lives in Alberta with her awesome husband and her super cute dog. She's addicted to home improvement shows, good coffee, and reading and writing about the steamier moments in life.

For more information about Ramona, check out her website at

www.ramonagray.ca

facebook.com/RamonaGrayBooks

twitter.com/RamonaGrayBooks

instagram.com/ramonagrayauthor

amazon.com/Ramona-Gray/e/B00OD26SAM

bookbub.com/profile/ramona-gray

ALSO BY RAMONA GRAY

Individual Books

The Escort

Saving Jax

The Assistant

One Night

Sharing Del

Filthy Appeal

Forbidden Bliss

Shadow Security Series

Dead of Night

Edge of Night

Dark of Night

Undeniable Series

Undeniably His

Undeniably Hers

Undeniably Theirs

Undeniable Series Boxset

Working Men Series

The Mechanic

The Carpenter

The Bartender

The Welder

The Electrician

The Landscaper

The Firefighter

The Cop

The Paramedic

Working Men Series Bundles

Working Men Series Books One to Three

Working Men Series Books Four to Six

Working Men Series Books Seven to Nine

Other World Series

The Vampire's Kiss (Book One)

The Vampire's Love (Book Two)

The Shifter's Mate (Book Three)

Rescued By The Wolf (Book Four)

Claiming Quinn (Book Five)

Choosing Rose (Book Six)

Elena Unbound (Book Seven)

Other World Series Box Sets

Other World Series Books One to Three

Other World Series Books Four to Six